You Never Knew Me

A Novel

Marty Almquist

ISBN-13: 978-0-9852624-6-4

Although no one can go back and make a brand-new start, anyone can start from now and make a brand-new ending.

-- Carl Bard (attributed)

Paris is always a good idea.

-- Audrey Hepburn

Chapter 1

The bus ground to a halt with a soft hiss of brakes. Overhead, the Paris sky was a mottled gray, promising more rain showers. Jane heaved her bulky suitcase down the steps and into the damp street. It had held up well, showing its age with just a few small scuff marks. She'd used it fairly often in the early years of their marriage, but recently it had been gathering dust in the attic, hidden under miscellaneous boxes of Christmas decorations and Kallie's saved school projects.

As she guided it onto the sidewalk, she stopped and closed her eyes to concentrate on the smells—the rain falling on the wet pavement, and the aroma of baguettes and coffee from the nearby café. Sudden, sharp nostalgia, combined with the tension of the previous few days made her stumble slightly as she moved forward once more, focusing on each oversized wooden door she passed. Number 28 was dark green and looked freshly painted. Glancing down at Angela's instructions, she punched the code into the keypad, and was relieved when she heard a buzz as the latch released. Using her shoulder to wedge open the heavy door, she lifted her bag over the metal frame of the entryway onto the cobblestones inside. She found herself in a wide passageway and glancing to her left, she could see a winding stairway through a glass door, but Angela's note had said to continue through the courtyard to the doorway on the far side.

As her suitcase clattered loudly across the cobblestones, she grimaced, hoping she wasn't waking any neighbors. Punching in a second code, she entered a small, musty hallway that led to a tiny elevator. She held her breath as it creaked to a stop on the second floor, the metal door folding back reluctantly. On the small landing, she turned to the door on the left, slid the strangely shaped key into the lock, and felt another rush of relief when the door clicked open. Her shoulders slumped at the sudden release of tension, and she stepped inside. She had arrived.

Moving through the dimness toward a set of shuttered windows, she fumbled for a moment with the unfamiliar catches, then opened the windows wide, letting the cool, wet air fill the room. She could see patches of watery sunlight trying to break through the dark clouds.

From her second-floor vantage point, her view was of the tops of the umbrellas of the passersby and occasional glimpses of disembodied legs and feet. A wave of exhaustion hit her, and she sagged against the rail, resting for just a moment before her growling stomach reminded her she needed to buy food before she let herself sleep.

A quick tour showed her a bedroom beyond the living room as well as one on the other side of the entryway, an immaculate blue and white bathroom, and finally a short hallway leading to a compact kitchen. Canvas shopping bags hung from a hook in the hallway, and after a quick glimpse into the fridge and pantry, she grabbed the largest bag, threw in the key, her phone and her wallet, and headed out, stopping briefly at the bottom of the stairs to send a quick text to

Angela.

> *I've arrived safe and sound. Big hugs to your aunt and tell*
> *her the apartment's perfect.*

Twenty minutes later, she was back and seated at the small dining table tucked next to the living room windows. She closed her eyes and bit down on the crunchy *céreale* baguette. It was a ritual from childhood—testing her senses of taste and smell to identify each ingredient in whatever she was eating. Today's was easy—sweet butter and tart raspberry jam, contrasting with the savory sunflower and sesame seeds in the baguette, followed by the sharp, slightly bitter coffee.

Looking out at the gently falling rain, she tried to empty her mind, focusing on the bright red geraniums filling the window boxes across the street. Instead, her final discussion with Jack replayed itself like a bad movie.

Kallie had just left for New York to start her first job, and Jane had put on a brave face, happy and proud of her daughter while simultaneously mourning the loss of her baby girl.

To distract herself, Jane had turned, as usual, to the comfort of cooking, finding quiet joy in each step of the process: from the visit to her local butcher; to placing the heavily spiced chicken into her iron skillet surrounded by vegetables from the local farmer's market. Jack had promised to be home promptly at eight and she remembered feeling the first stirrings of excitement at the thought of sharing her ideas about their future.

She'd turned as he entered the kitchen, a cocktail in each hand.

"Thank you," she'd said, smiling. He'd made hers just the way she liked it with an extra slice of lemon.

They'd sat in companionable silence at the breakfast bar, quietly sipping their drinks and looking out across the manicured lawn, but Jane noticed Jack seemed restless. He opened his mouth a couple of times as if to speak, but instead lapsed back into silence.

What was going on with him? she wondered. She waited for a moment more, then reached into her apron pocket, pulling out a crumpled piece of paper. He started when she touched his arm to hand it to him, looking confused as he unfolded it and squinted at the faded writing. "What's this?"

"The list we made on our honeymoon of all the places we wanted to go one day."

"You've kept it all these years?" She could hear the note of incredulity in his voice.

"You said our first priority should be starting a family and building our careers and save traveling for later. Well. It's now later."

Jack was silent for a long moment, returning his gaze to the darkening sky, and Jane's stomach clenched. Why was he not saying anything?

"It's been in my jewelry box," she continued. "And now Kallie is on her way, so I figured why not pull it out? There are lots of options," she continued brightly, knowing she was babbling but afraid of his continued silence. "And I thought it would help both of us feel less sad about Kallie leaving.

"My first choice would be Paris, of course. I'd love to show you my old haunts. And spring is a great time to visit. The bright green of the chestnut trees, the first daffodils...." She trailed off.

Nothing.

"Jack, please look at me. What's wrong? If you'd rather not go there, that's fine. We can figure out somewhere else."

He finally turned to face her, and she was shocked by how sad he looked, the worry lines etched deeply into his cheeks. He reached into his coat pocket and handed her an official-looking document.

She unfolded it slowly, dread making her hands tremble slightly. It was a signed Purchase & Sale Agreement for a house to be built in a project called "The Landing" in New Hampshire. "I don't understand."

"It's the newest development we've been working on with Jack Tillis, that residential builder we do a lot of business with." He paused. "The guys at the office all agree it's a great spot to retire. I'm not quite ready for that yet, but I figured we could start spending our summers there." Seeing her expression, his tone became defiant. "That's where *I* want to go."

Jane's heart was pounding, her mouth dry. "You want to go to New Hampshire?" she spat, her confusion giving way to anger. "Where we've gone every year since Kallie was born? That's your idea of a fun adventure?" She clenched her fists, willing herself to stay calm. "And before we talk about how crazy that idea is, let's go back a step. You bought a *house lot* in New Hampshire? Without talking to me?" She knew she sounded slightly hysterical.

Jack's voice, when he spoke again, was so quiet Jane had to lean forward to hear him.

"Yes, I bought a house lot. And I've been talking about doing it for six months, but you never listen when I'm saying something you don't want to hear."

He reached up to rub his forehead. "Jane, I'm tired of you not listening, and I'm tired of trying to be who you want me to be. I'm not interested in traveling. I've never been interested in traveling. I don't even remember making that list. It was probably after we'd had a few drinks. Just a make-believe game to get a laugh."

"What are you talking about? I remember that night very clearly. We talked about our future, and we spent a long time discussing it. Where we'd go first, and when."

"I don't remember any of that. And traveling has always been *your* dream, not mine. I've tried to have a longer conversation about this, but as soon as I raise any objections, you shut me out. Well, I'm done with keeping quiet."

Jane was stunned. Did she shut him out? No, she always listened. And she'd always let him have his way. She would ask about trips but never pushed when he said no.

"Jack, you can't mean that. You said we had to wait, and that made total sense, but I never heard you say you didn't want to do it at all."

"Don't you get it? I love New England and feel comfortable here. I have everything I need. I don't need to go anywhere else."

"I feel comfortable here, too, but that doesn't mean I don't want to see other places."

"Well, that's where we differ."

The whole situation felt unreal, like she was caught in a horrible dream. "I had no idea you were so unhappy."

"That's the point, Jane. I'm *not* unhappy. I love our life in Boston. I always have. You're the one who wants more." He took a large gulp of his drink. "With Kallie starting her own life, I think it's time for us to stop pretending." He paused. "If our life here isn't enough for you, I'm sorry." He swirled his drink, the clinking of the ice cubes unnaturally loud in the heavy silence.

After another long moment, he said, "Maybe we just need to rethink everything." Looking up finally to meet her gaze, he added, "Maybe we should get a divorce."

Jane pushed off her stool, dimly hearing it crash

behind her. Blindly stumbling up the stairs, she collapsed onto the bed. *What in the hell had just happened?*

Chapter 2

Jane pulled her sweater closer as she ventured out the next morning. Paris weather was definitely not as warm as she'd thought it would be in late May. The corner café beckoned with warmth and light, and Jane couldn't resist. She was tucked into a snug corner and given a menu by a stylish woman who introduced herself as Sylvie LeClerc, the owner. She was the epitome of French elegance, with blond hair framing a beautifully made-up face. Her blue eyes twinkled above a gorgeous Hermés silk scarf which was of course knotted beautifully. After she glided away to greet more guests, Jane took a surreptitious look around.

To her left was a man with horn-rimmed glasses, a thick scarf wrapped around his neck. He was slim, with well-worn jeans and brightly colored socks that peeked out over his glossy leather shoes. His novel was perched precariously at the edge of his table, on the brink of losing its competition for space with his espresso and croissant. On Jane's other side was a couple who looked like they'd stopped for breakfast on their way to work, the man in a well-tailored dark suit and red tie, the woman in a bold, patterned dress with a silk scarf artfully draped over it, and very high heels. Jane smiled to herself as Sylvie set down her *café crème* and croissant. She was definitely not in Boston anymore.

Thoughts of Boston brought everything flooding back, and she took a quick sip of her coffee around the sudden lump in her throat. It still felt unreal, her brain refusing to accept what she'd heard, her emotions veering from anger to frustration to disbelief.

The morning after Jack's stunning pronouncement she'd marched into HR and announced she had a personal emergency and would need to take a month off. She didn't even know where she'd come up with the timeframe. It just came out of her mouth, and she'd gone with it. In a fog, she'd ignored the shocked look of those around her as she delegated her workload and signed all the necessary papers, walking out the door as soon as she could to meet Angela at their favorite bar. She'd cried and raged in equal measure, giving her best friend all the details she'd not been able to include in her short, stunned text the night before.

Angela had provided tissues and a shoulder to cry on, and they'd agreed Jane needed to get out of town and as far away as possible from the whispers and veiled looks that would begin as soon as anyone in the country club circle figured out what her 'personal emergency' really was.

So, now that she was here, how was she going to spend her time? In her hurry to escape, she hadn't even considered what she might do to fill the empty hours. In Boston, work obligations, social commitments and her non-profit work gave her very little time for herself, but here the hours stretched ahead of her into a blank emptiness.

Since she hadn't been back to Paris since college, she knew she wanted to visit old favorite haunts, but then what? Jane picked up her phone to scroll through the email Angela had forwarded from her aunt, listing her favorite museums, restaurants, and activities around the city. Skimming the list, her attention was caught by two websites offering cooking classes.

She'd first learned to cook with her grandmother at age six, and throughout her life, preparing food and sharing it was when she was happiest. It had also become her escape—a way to set aside the stresses of work or home life and instead immerse herself in a task that she could control and one with a delicious conclusion.

Pulling up the first website, she found a class offered in three days cooking an entire meal featuring *coq au vin*. Now that sounded interesting. Most of the courses focused on just one item like bread or dessert. And it was something she'd never made. She quickly filled out the form and within seconds had a confirmation email. Figuring out the logistics of getting there would be a welcome distraction from the larger questions buzzing around her brain.

She noticed a missed text from Kallie from the night before, but it was just a photo showing the view from her new apartment. No need for more response than a thumbs up and heart emoji. Jane gazed at it for a moment. She hadn't wanted to worry Kallie with her abrupt departure, so she hadn't said anything. Angela suggested they say they'd decided to have a spontaneous girls' trips to Paris, but she didn't know if Kallie would believe it. Well, if not, Jane would figure something else out—if only the rest of it were as easy.

Chapter 3

When Fiona had departed from Liverpool that morning, everything around her had matched her somber mood. The thick layer of clouds overhead in muted shades of gray; the dull exteriors of buildings stained with years of smoke and soot and in need of a fresh coat of paint. The month since losing her Mum, she'd been in a fog, going through her daily routine on auto pilot. Now suddenly here she was in Paris, squinting in the bright sunshine, the blue sky a cloudless backdrop to rows of cream-colored buildings.

And the people. Not scurrying along, heads bowed, but instead walking with heads held high, a cigarette often dangling loosely from a gesticulating hand. And they were so elegant. Women in short skirts or tight jeans, each with a large handbag and high heels, the men in beautifully tailored suits, or faded, tight jeans and slim-cut, collared shirts. They all had narrow, handsome faces and inordinate amounts of beautiful dark hair. Fiona felt gawky and oversized. She was used to being taller than most of her friends, but here she felt like a giant. For a moment she felt panic threaten to overwhelm her, but she pushed it aside. It would all be fine. The hotel, airfare and train tickets had all been part of the travel package. The flight from Liverpool had arrived in London on time and she'd found her way to St Pancras to catch the Eurostar to Paris. Now all she had to do was find her way to the hotel.

Despite her internal bravado, she felt a relieved sense of accomplishment when she pushed open the door to the hotel thirty minutes later, her Paris Street map clutched in her hand. The woman at the desk looked up expectantly.

"May I help you?" she asked in perfect English, and Fiona let out a relieved sigh.

The travel package also included a cookery class, but it was not scheduled until the following day, so with no immediate plans, Fiona unpacked then wandered across the street to a café overflowing with patrons, hoping the crowd was a good indicator of the quality of the food. She was not disappointed. Her delicious *salade niçoise* took her back to her time years before when she'd come to Paris for a short business course. She sat with her face lifted to the sun, then opened her eyes to enjoy the people-watching. Why had she not been back? That was an easy one. The factory. Her family obligations. But she wouldn't think about that right now. She had a whole week stretching in front of her to live a different life. To think about art, and music, and to just sit in the sun. And she'd start with a trip to Sacré Coeur and say a prayer for her Mum.

The next morning, instead of her normal tea and toast, she ordered a *café crème* and croissant, feeling very cosmopolitan. Sitting in her same spot as the day before, she was amazed at the changing tableau of people of all ages and nationalities hurrying past. She'd brought her book to read but found the passing show much more entertaining. A quick look at the map told her the walk to the cooking class would take about thirty minutes, so at 11:30, she reluctantly paid her check and set off. Everywhere around her was noise and bustle, a world of people who seemed to all have places to go and things to do. Fiona found herself joining the flowing current of humanity, with an occasional stop to admire the creative, colorful window displays she passed.

She'd never been brave enough to take a cookery class at home, but this week felt like the perfect moment to try. It was in English, of course—she'd double checked before booking—but even so, she felt a bit nervous. Her Mum had never been much of a cook, and even after Fiona was on her own, she'd never felt the need to move beyond the basic recipes from her childhood. It was easier to just go down to the local pub. She hoped her classmates wouldn't get frustrated with her lack of skills.

She smiled, thinking back to how this adventure had begun. Because the office internet was so much faster than hers at home, she'd started staying late to take "virtual" voyages to exotic destinations to escape the sadness that overwhelmed her each time she visited her mother. A week after her mother died, a popup caught her attention— "Last Minute Bookings to Paris Means Great Savings!" – and she'd started clicking through a hypothetical seven-day trip. When it showed her the total and asked for her personal information, she'd filled out the form, and suddenly, without making a conscious decision—or at least she didn't *think* she'd made one—she pressed 'Buy.'

She'd sat back, her heart pounding, realizing suddenly what she'd done. She couldn't quite believe it. It was not carefully thought through. It was irresponsible. It was spontaneous. And she was *never* spontaneous. But it *was* exactly the sort of thing her Mum would have urged her to do. Mum, who had lived vicariously through travel shows on the telly. Mum, who had never gone anywhere because she was married to a man who was married to the family business.

Fiona was brought back to the present by a brightly colored scarf in a shop window. It was draped fashionably over the shoulders of the mannequin in the window, and she stopped, mesmerized. She absolutely loved it but told herself she'd look ridiculous in something so exotic. With a sigh, she started walking again, then stopped. Hadn't she just told herself this trip was all about new and positive experiences?

She opened the door and after a conversation of hand gestures interspersed with a few heavily accented words on both sides, Fiona walked out, feeling like a completely different person. The saleswoman had even showed her how to tie it so that it fell in graceful folds down the front of her blouse.

Could that reflection in the café window she passed really be her? Yes, the same brown hair, the same deep brown eyes, the same freckles across her nose, but there was new color in her cheeks, and an unexpected gleam of confidence in her eye. She strode forward, grinning broadly.

Chapter 4

Fiona stopped for a moment outside the creamy limestone building to read the cheerful chalkboard sign in front announcing the day's classes. Stepping inside, she was greeted by a young woman standing beside a small, ornate desk. Her smooth, dark hair, cut into a fashionable bob, closely followed the line of her chin, and her blue eyes sparkled behind a pair of spiky orange glasses.

How do these Frenchwomen make elegance look so easy? Fiona thought with a pang of envy.

"*Bonjour, Madame.* You are 'ere for the cooking class?" She smiled and came forward to shake Fiona's hand. "I am Brigitte." Fiona found her French accent charming.

"*Bonjour.* Yes, I'm Fiona Braxton."

Brigitte glanced at her list and made a notation. "Follow me, *s'il vous plait.*" She turned and gracefully made her way along the hall to a door that opened into a large, bright, room which contained six narrow tables, each set with two neatly folded aprons and two stools. Large, professional-looking stovetops filled the far end of the room. A workspace island, with a mirror above it, stood in front of one of them.

Brigitte gestured for Fiona to choose a place for herself.

The two couples occupying the front tables seemed to know each other and were chatting quietly. Fiona nodded to them, then chose a spot in the second row. Overhearing their posh accents, she decided they must be from London.

The door opened again and a young woman who looked to be in her late twenties or early thirties entered, dressed in the same effortless style as Brigitte. She had on a short-sleeved printed top and a white cardigan over a pair of stylish jeans and ankle-high boots. Her straight blond hair was pulled back into a ponytail.

She approached Fiona, smiling, and offered her hand. "*Bonjour.* May I join you? I'm Véronique Moreau."

Fiona shook her hand, slouching slightly, self-conscious of her height even in her flats.

"Fiona?" The way she said it made it sound softer and more feminine. "It is nice to meet you. What brings you to Paris?"

"I'm on a package tour from Liverpool."

"Ah, I have never been there. That is where the Beatles were from, *n'est-ce pas*?"

Fiona nodded, grinning.

"I would like to visit there one day."

"What brings you to a cooking class in English?"

"It's because of my job," answered Véronique as she tied on her apron. "I work for Bon Gout, a small independent grocery store chain, and we are opening a store in London. I have been asked to oversee it." Her eyes were bright with excitement.

"Congratulations!"

"*Merci.* It is a lot of responsibility. I told *mon patron* — my boss — that the class would give me the chance to interview prospective customers about what foods and wines they would like our store to sell."

Movement at the back of the class made them both turn to see a slim woman hesitating at the doorway. Her straight, brown hair was slightly windblown, and her skillfully applied makeup highlighted her large brown eyes and wide mouth. She was dressed in a pair of designer jeans, a long-sleeved sky-blue linen tunic, and glossy leather boots. Her outfit was understated but obviously expensive.

Her gaze swept the room, and when Fiona and Véronique both smiled, she moved to join them.

"Hello." Her voice was soft, her accent American. "I'm Jane Longworth."

Fiona reached her hand across the table. "I'm Fiona, and this is Véronique." She glanced at Véronique, hoping she hadn't mangled the pronunciation too badly, but Véronique didn't look offended. Fiona continued. "I want to confess right up front that I'm not a very good cook, but I'll try my best."

"I'm sure they'll give us detailed instructions for everything," Jane said, smiling.

"*Excusez-moi,*" a voice interrupted, and they turned to face the young man clad in a white apron and chef's hat standing at the front of the class. When the conversations had quieted, he continued. "*Bonjour.* My name eez Chef Jacques and I have brought you delicious produce from the Place Monge farmer's market zis morning to cook and, of course, to eat." Soft laughter and smiles rippled around the room. "As you know, we will be preparing an entire meal, so the class will be divided into four groups with each focusing on one part of the meal. Please come up to the front and I will explain the dishes we will be preparing."

"I was wondering how we were going to cook everything," Jane whispered as they moved forward.

Chef Jacques waited until they were all standing

around him, then continued. "The meal will start with a Dubarry, which is a cauliflower soup, followed by the *coq au vin*, with glazed turnips and carrots, and mashed potatoes. That will be followed by a cheese course, and finally a Peach Melba *pour le dessert*. You do not need to take notes because we will send you all the recipes." Several people looked relieved. "Who would like to make the soup?"

Jane looked over at Véronique and Fiona, who both nodded, and she raised her hand.

"Do any of you know why it is called a Dubarry?" They shook their heads. "The last mistress to King Louis XV, Madame Dubarry, liked cauliflower, and she was so charming the chef for the court named the soup after her. Quite a romantic story, *non?* And *le chou-fleur*, the cauliflower, and the leeks, *les poireaux*, are from the market this morning."

Everyone smiled, and he turned toward the next basket on the counter. "Next are *les navets et les carottes*, the turnips and carrots." One of the couples from London volunteered for that and he said, "You will be using a *cuillère à pomme parisienne*, a melon baller in English, to prepare them up before you sauté them."

"The next group will be working on the mashed potatoes which will be prepared Robuchon style. Is anyone familiar with this technique?" A shake of heads. "It is a method named after Chef Joel Robuchon and you will see that it requires lots of butter." He smiled at their laughter and the other London couple from the front of the room raised their hands. He now moved to the last basket.

"Finally, the Peach Melba, a delicious dessert made with peaches, *les pêches*, a raspberry sauce, *coulis de framboise*, and vanilla ice cream, *glace vanille*. We will also be adding grated almonds on top for a leetle crunch." Jane and Fiona grinned at his pronunciation. The final two couples, one

British and one American who'd been at the back of the room, moved forward, the women giggling. Fiona thought they looked very young.

"There is a written copy of the instructions for your dish at your station and I will take turns working with each of you as we all prepare the meal. Please feel free to walk around on your own to observe what others are doing."

Everyone moved to their assigned stations, and Jane was the first to speak after studying the recipe.

"Fiona, do you want to cut up the leek and sauté it? I'll chop the cauliflower. Véronique, can you go get the milk we need and the saffron? And a hand mixer, to blend it at the end." She stopped, looking suddenly sheepish. "Oops, sorry, didn't mean to sound so bossy. My husband says I always think I'm in charge." Fiona noticed Jane suddenly seemed tense and her smile looked forced.

Véronique laughed. "That is not necessarily a bad thing. Someone has to manage things, right? What about you, Fiona? Are you bossy?"

"I'm not sure. I *try* to manage our sales team at work but getting them to follow any sort of instructions is like herding cats." They all laughed, and Fiona noticed Jane seemed to relax slightly.

Chef Jacques clapped his hands for attention. "*Pardon.* I just realized I did not tell you about the most important course, the *coq au vin.*" He smiled. "As you may know, *coq au vin* takes many hours to cook, so since we do not have room for everyone to stay here with us tonight," several people laughed, "we have come up with another solution." He looked questioningly at Brigitte, who responded with a shrug, and he looked toward the door, glancing at his watch nervously.

As if on cue, the door swung open, and a man strode in with a large silver chafing dish covered in foil. As he made his way to the front, the enticing aroma of roasted chicken and red wine filled the room.

"Ah, *voila!*" Chef Jacques looked relieved. The two men spoke quietly, and then the large dish was placed into the oven. They turned to face the group, and Chef Jacques said, "Class, here it is, prepared by my good friend, Chef Bernard." Bernard had thick dark, curly brown hair and wore a white chef's jacket over his jeans. Various members of the class smiled or waved in greeting before returning to their preparations.

Fiona turned to ask Jane a question and noticed her gaze was fixed toward the two men. Fiona glanced back toward the front but didn't notice anything unusual. When she looked back at Jane, her head was down, seemingly intent on her task, but Fiona could see her cheeks were bright pink. She and Véronique exchanged a questioning look.

"Jane, can you hand me the whisk?" There was no response and Fiona spoke again, more loudly. "Jane? The whisk?"

Jane started suddenly, her eyes turning toward Fiona. "Sorry, sorry. Here you go."

"Jane, you seem distracted," Véronique said, raising one eyebrow and grinning. She followed Jane's gaze toward the door that was just closing. "What's going on?"

"Nothing. Sorry. I was listening to what Chef Jacques was saying about the *coq au vin.*"

"Oh, of course." Véronique winked at Fiona.

The room filled again with the quiet hum of activity and muffled conversations.

At 1:30, Chef Jacques declared that all was ready, and they should all walk back to the front room. A large table had been set with colorful Provencal napkins, white porcelain plates, sparkling glassware, and antique silverware. Jane's stomach clenched for a moment as she thought about all the beautiful dinner parties she and Jack had hosted, using the special bone china dishware she'd inherited from her grandmother.

After they were seated, Brigitte appeared, carrying a large tureen, steam wafting from the top. Fiona, Jane and Véronique looked at each other with pride as their classmates tasted the soup and proclaimed it to be delicious. Next came the *coq au vin*, served with the vegetables and the potato purée, and everyone again declared the cooking a success, asking Chef Jacques to send thanks to Bernard.

Brigitte then brought out smaller plates and an enormous cheese platter. "Some of you may not know that Véronique has been in charge of the cheese department at Bon Gout the last several years." She turned to face Véronique. "Would you do us the honor of describing the various cheeses on offer?"

Véronique looked surprised and pleased. "*Merci, Chef Jacques et Brigitte.* It would be my pleasure." She moved forward. "Before I begin, may I ask a small favor?' At Brigitte's nod, she turned to face the rest of the group. "As some of you know, Bon Gout is opening a store in London soon and it would be very helpful for me if you would let me know which cheeses are your favorites once you've tried them today. I would also be happy to hear of any other French products you are interested in, and I will do my best to stock them for you. With your help, I hope to have the best store in London!"

There was applause and smiles, and as Brigitte opened another bottle of wine, the conversation became more animated, and the laughter louder.

Brigitte then brought out the Peach Melba and coffee, and conversation turned to what everyone was enjoying about their respective visits to Paris. Reluctantly, after another thirty minutes, people stood and, with friendly banter and promises to stay in touch, the group dispersed.

"I'm looking forward to comparing the *coq au vin* recipe with my mother's," Véronique said as they gathered their things and moved toward the front door.

Chef Jacques shook their hands as they walked out. "I will look forward to visiting the London store."

"I will send you an invitation to the grand opening. Thank you so much for everything."

As they reached the sidewalk, Fiona said, "I don't want this day to end. Do either of you have time for coffee or another glass of wine?"

"I don't need more wine, but I'd love a coffee," Jane said. "How about you, Véronique?"

"*Absolument.* I took the day off from work and I intend to stay away from all that chaos until tomorrow."

Ten minutes later, they'd found a café and were sipping espressos.

"It smells so different here," Jane said, her eyes closed. "Even if I couldn't see anything, I'd know I'm in Paris, not Boston."

"What are the differences?" Fiona closed her own eyes for a moment, then opened them again.

"Cigarette smoke for one. We don't have all these smokers. Then there's the coffee smell. Our coffee doesn't smell nearly as sharp as the expresso. We do have car exhaust, of course, though not out in Wellesley where I live." She paused, breathing in more sharply. "We do *not* have anywhere to get *steak frites* that smell like that," she said, pointing to the couple two tables over. "I'm so full, but my mouth is still watering."

"I wish we had places where you can sit outside like this in Liverpool," Fiona murmured, her head tilted toward the sun.

They sat quietly for a moment, then Jane spoke again. "On a different topic, I know you both said you liked the class, but I was disappointed in one aspect of it."

Fiona looked over. "Really? I thought they did a good job."

"They did on the dishes we actually cooked, but I signed up because it said we were making *coq au vin*."

"That's a good point, though I thought his reasons made sense. It does take a long time to make. And they are sending us the recipe."

"I know, and if I'd thought it through, I would have realized that. Still...."

Véronique smiled mischievously. "I guess you'll just have to go find that Chef Bernard and ask him to give you a private lesson."

Jane sputtered, grabbing a napkin to wipe her mouth.

Fiona giggled. "Jane don't even try to deny you fancied him. We saw how you couldn't take your eyes off him."

"What are you talking about?" Jane protested. "I was trying to listen to what they were saying about the *coq au vin*."

"You just keep telling yourself that," Véronique said, smiling.

Jane tried to look indignant, then shrugged. "Okay, I admit he's attractive. But I'm a married woman. I'm not supposed to notice that sort of thing."

Fiona looked at them with mock solemnity. "My mum always said it was okay to look, just not sample the merchandise." She and Véronique looked at each other and burst into laughter.

Véronique's phone, which was on the table in front of her, buzzed and lit up, and she glanced down. "*Oh, merde*, it's from my assistant." She looked at the text, frowning. "She says it's about London and it's urgent." She sighed. "Apparently, my office can't survive without me even for one day. Fiona, you're just here this week, right? I'd love to try to get together before you go home. Maybe even introduce you to my husband, Jean-Pierre."

"I leave Saturday."

"Okay, let's connect on WhatsApp and I'll send a text when I know what works." She swung her purse over her shoulder and left with a wave.

Jane turned to Fiona. "So, what do you have planned for the rest of the week?"

"Tomorrow I'm thinking of riding one of those 'Hop-On Hop-Off' buses. Want to join me?"

"Thanks, but I know the city pretty well already, so I think I'll pass. If you want to go to an exhibit or a meal, I'd love to do that."

"Have you been here often?"

"Not recently." Jane looked sad, and Fiona wondered why. "The last time was during my junior year of college back in 1992."

"That's funny. I was here, then, too, on a three-month business course. I think I still want to ride the bus to get a good overview of where everything is. Let's check in with each other later in the afternoon, or if that doesn't work, try to get together later in the week."

"That sounds great."

They paid the check and Jane, with a wave, set off in search of a bookstore she'd heard about. Fiona wandered back toward her hotel, feeling completely relaxed. She came to a bridge and stopped halfway across, gazing at the swirling water below. Behind her a lone musician serenaded anyone who would listen on his guitar, hoping for a coin or two in his hat. She looked up at the slowly darkening sky and though she knew it was crazy, she felt her Mum smiling down. This trip had been a really good idea. Everything in Paris felt so removed from her life in Liverpool.

As she started walking again, she realized *she* felt like a different person, too. The trepidation she'd felt yesterday when she'd arrived had diminished with each small victory— figuring out how to use the metro; getting through the cookery class without making a fool of herself; even just daring to eat in a restaurant alone. Small successes in practice, but enormous boosts to her self-confidence.

Who knew? She might even dare to try making the cauliflower soup for herself when she got back to Liverpool. She stopped suddenly and several people muttered as they brushed past her. Liverpool. Her brother, Kevin, who wanted to talk about the future. Kevin, whose whole life was the factory, according to his now-ex-wife. But was that what *she* wanted?

Chapter 5

Back at the office, Véronique read through the email one more time before pushing 'send,' and only then letting her breath out with a large sigh. She'd been irritated at Marianne for texting her, but it was good she'd come in.

Standing, she glanced at her watch, then made her way to the lounge to get a coffee. She smiled as David fell into step beside her. He'd started at Bon Gout the same week she had, but he was on the technology side, overseeing the website and various social media platforms. Véronique had quickly grown to depend on him as her sounding board and perfect confidante when she needed to vent.

"*Salut.* I thought you had the day off?"

"I did, but Marianne texted me in a panic."

"What about? Wait. Let me guess. Something with the London store?"

"Yep. There's a long lead time for getting some of the permits and it turns out I needed to get the paperwork for one of them in by the end of business today."

"And you didn't know that?" David said in a mock serious tone. "Shame on you! Off playing hooky when you should be diligently filing paperwork."

Véronique punched him playfully in the arm. "I wasn't playing hooky. I was gathering market research data." She told him about the cooking class as they poured their coffees and found a corner table. "I will say I was pleasantly surprised how quickly my English came back, though when I chatted with the younger couples, I really felt old. They kept talking about how 'dope' everything was, and every time I looked over at their table, they were snapping photos of each other cooking. I like Instagram but they took it to a whole new level."

"Not being a crazy social media hound doesn't make you old," he said. "What about everyone else?"

"Most people, including the two women I partnered with, Jane and Fiona, were in their forties and fifties, I think. Jane is from Boston, and Fiona is from Liverpool. I really had fun, and it was a relief to not talk about babies or home decoration, which is *all* our friends seem to do right now."

"C'mon, it can't be that bad, and those are things young couples *do* talk about."

"I know, but it just makes Jean-Pierre get amorous and starry-eyed and full of not-so-subtle hints that we should start a family."

David nudged her arm. "Amorous and starry-eyed isn't so bad...."

"Stop! Not if it's for the wrong reasons. Speaking of kids, how's Mathilde?"

David glanced at his watch. "She's good. It's my turn to pick her up from ballet so I need to get out of here in fifteen minutes or so. Speaking of which, it's still officially your day off. You need to get out of here, too."

"I know. I'll just take a quick look through the inventory updates since I'm here. Saves me coming in early tomorrow."

"Why do you have to come in early tomorrow?" Camille asked from the doorway, a waft of her heavily floral perfume proceeding her. Her blond, streaked hair swept off her forehead in what Véronique was sure was supposed to be a 'natural' wave but to Véronique looked stiff as a board. Camille had started the same day as Véronique and David, but from that first day Véronique couldn't stand her. It was the way she dressed, with her stiletto heels and bright colored tops that were just slightly lower cut than was professional, her nails that were always a glossy red or pink, her lipstick and make up that looked more appropriate for an evening soirée. To Véronique, everything about her was over the top and blatantly fake, but Camille had been very successful and in fact had just been promoted to Director of Marketing for the entire company.

Véronique felt her stomach clench, but she forced herself to smile. "Hey, Camille. We were talking about the London store."

"How's it going?"

"Great."

"Glad to hear it. I overheard someone talking about how many problems your team was having getting all the logistics figured out."

Véronique counted to ten, biting her lip to keep from firing back an angry response. She was amazed at how calm she sounded when she answered. "Not at all. It's been more complicated than opening in France, that's for sure, but we're fine. You just make sure you get us the visibility and press coverage when the time comes."

Camille's face tightened for a moment, then she waved her hand through the air dismissively. "I've got that all arranged, don't worry. I guess being here all hours is fine since

Jean-Pierre is working all the time, too, on that big pitch, right?"

Again, Véronique found herself biting her tongue. "We're all at that point in our careers, aren't we? Working crazy hours, I mean."

"Gives you an excuse to hang out here with David, so that's not all bad, right?" Now Camille's smile became complicit and Véronique blushed, then was furious at herself.

"David's just heading out, actually, to pick up his *daughter*, right David?" Véronique said pointedly.

"Yes, I am in fact." David rose from his chair and started for the door.

"I've got a client dinner, so I'm headed out, too." Camille said, turning quickly and slipping her arm into his. "I'll walk down with you."

Véronique felt her jaw clench and forced herself to relax. Camille wasn't worth getting upset over and she was right about one thing. Véronique *had* been staying way too late every night. And it didn't help that recently she and Jean-Pierre seemed to bicker whenever they *were* together.

Remembering her discussion with Fiona and Jane about a possible dinner, she took out the phone and dialed Jean-Pierre's number. "*Salut.* Can you leave work early on Wednesday? I want you to meet the two women I met in class today and make them dinner."

"I... think so."

He didn't sound confident and Véronique snapped, "Seriously? You've been there late every night for weeks."

"Okay, okay. I'll clear it with Martin tomorrow."

"Perfect." Hanging up, she knew she sounded short, and for a moment felt guilty, but then shrugged to herself and sent a quick text to Jane and Fiona.

Dinner at my apartment is on! I'll meet you at the

Abbesses metro Wednesday at 7:30.

Now all she had to do was figure out what to cook and cross her fingers Jean-Pierre made it home at a reasonable hour.

Chapter 6

The next morning, Jane grabbed her purse and bounded down the stairs. She'd slept deeply and felt like she was finally on French time. After grabbing a copy of the weekly magazine Véronique had recommended to find out what was happening in the city, *L'Officiel des Spectacles*, she headed to the corner café.

"*Bonjour*, Sylvie."

"*Bonjour*, Jane. *Un café crème?*"

"*Oui, merci beaucoup.*"

Before going to bed the night before, she'd made a list of 'to do' items, and the first item was to come up with ideas of exhibits and concerts she could share with Fiona.

Jane flipped through the music section and immediately turned down the page corner at a listing for a Vivaldi concert at Sainte Chapelle. That could be fun. She then found a couple of interesting exhibits, one at the D'Orsay museum and one at the Musée de Luxembourg and turned down the corners of those pages.

On the next page began a listing of current movies, and she smiled when she saw that several of the theaters she used to frequent as a student were still operating. One of her favorite things to do with her French boyfriend at the time was to go see American classic films from the 1940's. They'd met in a film noir class, and he shared her love for the black and white movies of that era. *Francois*. She could still picture him. Dark brown hair, a wry smile, and an intense gaze from bright blue eyes. He'd invited her back to his place after the third date—a tiny studio apartment on the top floor of an old Haussman-style building at the far edge of the fifth *arrondissement*.

Jane had loved it the moment she saw it. A Tiffany lamp perched on a tiny bedside table shed a soft glow on the single bed, which was tucked under a slanted ceiling. A rag rug on the floor and a scratched, pale green dresser with a hot plate on top were the only other furnishings and he'd hung a bright Indian blanket on one wall. She could see a profusion of plants on the tiny balcony.

Jane was brought back to the present by Sylvie setting down her croissant, and she set the magazine aside to gently pull it apart and take her first bite, closing her eyes briefly to savor the still warm, yeasty flavor.

She turned back to her list. The next item was finding a hostess gift to thank Véronique for inviting them to dinner at her apartment, and she already knew what she wanted to get. While perusing the bookshelves the night before, she'd found a book, in English, filled with detailed descriptions and colorful pictures of cheeses. It was obvious Angela's Aunt Bobbie had strong opinions based on the scrawled, playful, comments written in red ink next to obvious favorites, as well as multi-colored scraps of paper that served as bookmarks.

Holy Smoke!
Stinky but Delish!
Def Prefer 10-yr aged version

Even without the personal annotations, Jane felt sure Véronique would love a copy of the book itself, and she remembered several bookstores in the heart of the touristy Left Bank, that had decent English-language sections. As a student, she'd shopped there for textbooks and novels, but she felt sure they would also have cookbooks and reference books for the tourists who wandered the area each day.

Sylvie told her which bus to take and once she'd arrived at Place St Michel, she walked up to one of her favorites from her student days—*Gibert Joseph.* A friendly young man at the information counter gave her detailed directions but spoke so quickly she had to have him repeat it twice.

She also found herself noticing his thick, wild hair. *What was it with these French men?* It reminded her of the *coq au vin* chef. What was his name? Chef Bernard. That was right. She smiled thinking about how distracted she'd been by him. She'd even given him a secret nickname because of that disheveled hair. *Monsieur Bedhead.* Thank God she hadn't confessed *that* little tidbit to Fiona and Véronique, considering what a hard time they'd given her at the café.

Thanking the young man, she made her way to the escalator and with only one wrong turn, found the English-language section. Where to begin? She knew the author's name and had taken a picture of the book itself, but how did they organize this sort of reference book? By author? By title? By subject? She was afraid to ask for more help knowing it would result in more rapid-fire French.

She cocked her head sideways, looking at the titles and authors to see if she could figure it out and almost ran into someone standing in the aisle, deeply engrossed in a book he held in his hands.

"*Excusez-moi,*" Jane said, then gaped when she saw

who it was. Chef Bernard! What on earth was he doing here? She realized her mouth was hanging open and rapidly closed it.

He moved out of the way, apologizing and glancing briefly at her, then back again with a dawning recognition. He smiled—a slow, sexy smile that made the blood rush to her cheeks.

"*Bonjour.* You were in the cooking class." His English was very good, with only a slight accent.

"*Oui,* uh, yes." Her brain felt frozen.

He reached out to shake her hand. "I'm Bernard."

"Yes, Chef Bernard. Nice to see you again." Up this close, she could see he had deep brown eyes, with gold suns around each pupil.

"And you are?" he asked after a moment, his tone teasing.

"Oh, of course. I'm Jane. Sorry. I just can't get over what a funny coincidence it is to run into you like this."

"Paris is a small city in some ways," he said, his eyes sparkling. "I'm looking for a cookbook for a friend. What about you?"

"I'm looking for a book about cheeses." She pulled her phone out and showed him the picture she'd taken of Bobbie's copy.

"I know that one. Over here, I think." Bernard led her further along the shelf and after peering closer, he pulled out a copy. "Here it is."

"Are there two copies by any chance? I'm buying it as a gift, but I'd love one for myself as well."

"Let's see. Yes, there are. And here's one on wine and cheese pairings that I have at home that I find helpful. If you're interested."

"Thank you." Jane opened the second book and made

a pretense of looking at it, though she couldn't concentrate. "This looks great, thanks." Her heart had finally slowed to a more normal pace. She noticed her head came to just below his chin.

"Your English is very good," she stammered.

"*Merci*. My wife was English. I learned from her."

His wife. She felt her stomach drop. "You said you're buying a cookbook?"

"Yes." He held up the book in his hand. "It's written by the chef of *Le Chateaubriand*. Have you heard of it?" Jane shook her head. "It's a restaurant in the 11ᵗʰ *arrondissement*. My friend and I went there when he was in town. You should go if you have time. Are you looking for any other books?"

"No, that was it. Thank you for your help."

"My pleasure." They stood there awkwardly for a moment before Bernard put his book under his arm. "You must pay for them at the *caisses* on the ground floor. I can show you?"

"Thank you." She didn't see any reason to tell him she already knew that. They headed down the stairs and moved to adjacent check-out windows.

Jane took longer than Bernard to check out and was surprised to find him waiting for her outside. "Sorry. That was the first time I'd used my phone app to pay for something and I wasn't sure it would work here." Jane felt like she was babbling in her nervousness.

"No problem at all. Do you by any chance have time for a coffee?" At her hesitation, he added, "Sorry, maybe that was too forward. I was just wondering what you thought of the *coq au vin.*"

"Not forward at all. I'd love to talk to you about it." She smiled, and he grinned back, looking relieved.

"Perfect. I know a good spot near here."

As they walked up a couple of blocks Jane couldn't help thinking about Véronique and Fiona's teasing, and for a moment wondered if it was too weird to agree to have coffee with a perfect stranger. No, he was Chef Jacques' friend. It would be fine.

Bernard turned into a side street, and immediately the noise of the traffic muted. Two blocks further along, the street opened into a small square with a café on the far side. The waiter directed them to an empty outside table.

Bernard spoke first. "I apologize. This is a bit strange. I don't normally ask women I don't know to have coffee."

"And I don't normally accept offers like that, but it feels like we have a friend in common."

"Jacques. Yes, that's how I felt, too." They ordered and he turned back to her. "What did you think of the class?"

She hesitated. She didn't want to say anything negative, but it was what she was planning to write in the review online. "Honestly?"

"Yes, honestly."

"I liked it a lot except that I really wanted to make the *coq au vin* myself. That's a dish I've always wanted to learn to cook. Yours was delicious, by the way."

"Thank you and that's a valid point. He asked my advice, when he decided to offer a class that cooked an entire meal, and we both agreed there was no reasonable way to have you cook that, but he hoped that by cooking everything else, and getting the detailed recipe, it would be okay."

"I did sign up for it because it was an entire meal and not just bread or dessert actually."

"I'll tell him. That's helpful. Did you like cooking everything else?"

"Yes, and I will definitely cook them again at home."

"Speaking of that, those classes are usually full of Brits

and you're obviously not. Where are you from?"

"Boston."

"Oh, I love Boston."

"You've been there? I mean, it seems like the French usually go to New York, not Boston."

"My wife and I were in Boston for a conference. I loved the history and the small, twisty streets. Reminded me of home."

"Really? I don't think of Paris as having small twisty streets except up by Montmartre."

Bernard laughed. "I'm actually not from here. I'm from Dijon."

"I *love* Dijon."

"You've been there? It seems like Americans usually go to Paris, not Dijon," he teased, his eyes twinkling.

Jane laughed. "I lived in Paris when I was in college but as part of the program, I spent a month just outside of Dijon."

"Now I understand why your accent is so good."

Jane blushed. "Thank you. It's slowly coming back."

He was staring intently at her, and she hastily searched for something else to say. "The cookbook for your friend. Is he a chef?"

"No, he just loved the food we had that night. It was a tasting menu, and he was very impressed. When he heard the chef was putting out a cookbook, he asked me to keep an eye out for it. I'm sure he'll be able to find it in London at some point, but he didn't want to wait."

Bernard's phone buzzed and he glanced down, mumbling an expletive she couldn't quite hear. "I'm so sorry. I need to leave. There's a problem at work." He motioned for the waiter and reached in his pocket, pulling out a ten euro note.

Jane tried to protest, but Bernard waved her hand away. "My treat since I have to abandon you."

"Okay," she conceded, "but I'll treat you next time." Why did she say that? She doubted she'd ever see him again.

"I'll hold you to that." His gaze lingered on her for a moment, and his touch when he took her hand sent a little shock of electricity shooting up her elbow. "I hope we run into each other again soon." With a final wave and a smile, he turned and strode off.

She noticed he wasn't wearing a wedding ring.

But you are, she chided herself.

Chapter 7

Fiona, seated once again at what she now felt was "her" spot at the café, was re-thinking her plans for the day. She'd woken from a dream about her mother, and it had left a lingering sadness. She didn't feel like dealing with the crowds on the Hop-on, Hop-off bus. What should she do instead? She considered staying put and ordering another coffee, but sitting would lead to thoughts of Kevin and the factory. Maybe a long walk would keep the sadness and the worry at bay.

She decided to walk to Notre Dame to see the progress of the renovation. Like many people, she'd been glued to the telly the night of the dreadful fire, and she hoped seeing the renovation for herself would lift her melancholy mood.

She chose a route that took her to the back side of the cathedral since she'd read the plaza in front was still closed to the public. The narrow street was crowded with people gawking and taking pictures, and she gazed up, knowing what to expect but still feeling the shock course through her. The elaborate scaffolding highlighted the absence of the distinctive roof and spire, and she felt both a wave of sadness and a surge of hope at the evidence of its rebirth.

The char marks on the stone had not been visible on her small television screen, and their presence suddenly brought home the reality of what had happened.

The flying buttresses stood starkly outlined against the cloudless sky, strangely naked without the roof as a backdrop. She didn't remember them from her last trip and realized that like many tourists, she'd been focused on the elaborately carved wooden entrance doors and the two bell towers at the front.

Fiona found a park bench, then pulled out the guidebook she'd bought on her last visit twenty years before. The glossy cover photo showed Notre Dame in all its glory, and she touched it briefly in remembrance. The book had languished on a dusty shelf since that trip, but she'd run across it by chance a couple of months before, and she and her Mum had talked about the tragedy of the fire. Her mum had been deeply religious and very upset about it at the time.

She opened the book and lost herself in the church's history until brought out of her reverie by a crowd of noisy teenagers nearby. A quick glance at her phone showed her it was almost one and her stomach growled as if in response. It was time to leave her musings and focus on the practical question of finding something to eat. She meandered along the river past the *bouquinistes* -- the small stands containing dusty books, colorful posters, and the requisite tourist trinkets. Spotting a café with a view of the cathedral, she squeezed into an empty table between two groups of German tourists and ordered a bowl of French onion soup and a chilled glass of white wine. She raised her glass in a silent toast, then pulled her guidebook out to continue reading.

Forty minutes later, a screeching of brakes, followed by loud voices, startled her into looking up once more toward the quay, where a crowd of people on bicycles seemed to be surrounding the hood of a red car.

"What do you suppose happened?"

Fiona turned toward the voice—and the person attached to it—seated at a table two over from hers. She realized the German tourists had all departed and the tables were now mostly deserted.

The woman looked to be about her age, and her grey hair was cut in an unusual style—one side very short and the other side sweeping down over her forehead at a sharp angle. She was dressed casually in jeans and trainers, with a light jacket slung over her shoulders. Fiona immediately noticed her large green eyes, which at the moment looked highly amused. "Sounds like someone's not very happy."

Fiona was pleased to hear her British accent. "My French isn't good enough to know what it's about, but from that tone, I certainly wouldn't want to be involved." She stuck out her hand. "I'm Fiona Braxton."

"Emily Spenser." Emily's grip was firm. "I admit I'm curious. I'll investigate and be right back." Fiona closed her book, sliding a corner of her paper napkin in to hold her place as she waited for Emily's return.

A few moments later, Emily plopped down next to her. "It seems that a flashy red BMW decided to challenge a group of tourists on a bike tour, and the bike tour prevailed." She laughed, and Fiona found herself joining in. "I think the tour guide must have sped up to block the car, which was the sound of brakes we heard. The driver, a suave young Frenchman in bright orange trousers, was *not* happy. The tour leader, a feisty, short redhead, got right in his face, giving him back as good as she got." Emily paused, and with a mischievous smile added, "Do you want to go look? I'm happy to save your spot here."

Fiona shook her head. "No, it's probably vocabulary

that I'm better off without."

"Do you mind if I join you?"

"Not at all. Please do."

Emily moved her espresso to Fiona's table, hanging her oversized bag on her chair and pulling something out as she sat down. "That book you're reading is one of my favorites." She held up her own battered copy, its cover held in place with a large rubber band.

Fiona grinned. "I'll take the condition of yours as a good endorsement. I bought this the last time I visited Notre Dame many years ago but had never read it until now."

Emily's face turned serious. "Hard to see it looking like this, isn't it? I felt physically ill when I saw the spire falling."

"Were you here?"

"No, thank God."

"I felt the same way. I have such great memories of my last visit inside. I arrived just as a service was starting, and when the choir began singing, it gave me goosebumps. There was such a feeling of joy...." Fiona looked down, unable to continue.

"Notre Dame has that effect on lots of people, including me." They sat in companionable silence for a few moments.

"Are you here on holiday?" Emily asked, motioning to the waiter for another coffee.

"Yes, a one-week package tour. What about you?"

"I'm a research fellow at Oxford, so I'm here quite often for work. Right now, I'm working on a paper about the role that Notre Dame and the Catholic Church played during the French Revolution."

"Wow, that sounds interesting."

"Do you mean that or are you just being polite?"

Fiona laughed. "I mean it. Tell me more if you can keep it in layman's terms."

"You tempt me, but I will resist. You don't know what you're agreeing to." Emily laughed. "Suffice it to say that scrutiny and judgement by the Church, who knows everything about you and your family, combined with its obvious wealth and corruption, led to some very frustrated citizens."

"Put that way, I'd have revolted, too!" Fiona grinned.

"Exactly." Emily looked sheepish. "But enough about that. Tell me more about you and this trip. You said it's a package tour?"

"Yes, it was something I found through a random internet search, but I'm so glad I decided to come."

"Everyone should come to Paris as often as possible, in my opinion. What's included in it?"

"Transportation from Liverpool, seven nights at a hotel, a cookery class that I did yesterday, and a museum tour. I chose it because it wasn't set up as a large group doing everything together. The tour company lets you figure out what you want to do based on your own schedule."

"Interesting. I haven't heard of that, but it's a much better set up in my opinion. I'm not a fan of big tour groups."

"Me, neither." She decided she wouldn't confess she'd been planning to ride the Hop-On Hop-Off Bus that morning.

"So, when were you here the last time?"

"Twenty years ago, if you can believe it. I spent three months on a sort of business exchange between the UK and France. Now that I'm here, I can't believe I waited so long. Speaking of that, how can you do your research for your paper with all that's happened at Notre Dame?"

"The archives are in a separate building so they weren't affected by the fire, but it has delayed the process for sure. I'm here this week because I was finally able to set up interviews with their historians. My first meetings are tomorrow."

Emily motioned to the waiter for the bill, then turned. "That means I have one more free afternoon. I'd love to show you around this area, which is one of my favorites. Do you have time?"

"I'd love that." Fiona glanced at her phone. "I do need to text a friend from the cookery class because we said we might get together, but we didn't have any specific plans. Just give me a second." Fiona typed quickly, then put her phone away.

"Tell me more about the class," Emily said as they gathered their belongings. "I've never done anything like that, but I've always wanted to. What did you make? Did you get to eat what you cooked?" Emily continued to pepper Fiona with questions as they started walking.

They meandered through small, curving alleyways, and window shopped on the grand boulevards, stopping to read menus at restaurants they passed. It was exactly how Fiona liked to see a city, but after a couple of hours of cars honking, scooters buzzing by and growling buses, Fiona was starting to flag. "Do you mind if we stop and get a drink somewhere?"

"Not at all. Sorry—my family says I never know when to stop. C'mon, I know a place near here you'll like." She led Fiona down several side streets till they arrived at a small restaurant with brimming outdoor tables and an aroma of garlic and roasting meat that made Fiona's mouth water. Emily continued inside to a table in a quiet corner.

Once they were settled, Fiona gazed around, loving the large, hand-drawn maps covering the walls that showed different sections of Paris, the ink aged to a light brown. A banquette, covered in dark red velveteen, provided the seating for the tables along the back wall. The lamps over the banquette had just turned on, emitting a soft, orange glow over everything.

A waiter appeared at Emily's elbow, greeting her warmly in French, and Fiona was impressed with Emily's quick responses. Emily then turned to her. "What would you like?"

"I would love a lager. I don't know the French beers, though."

"Do you mind if I choose for you?"

"Not at all." Emily turned and quickly spoke again to the waiter who then hurried away.

"Thank you. Your French is really good. Is that from taking classes, or just from visiting so often?"

"A combination. I took classes for a while, and I belong to a French club that meets once a month."

"That's a good idea. I wonder if I could find something like that in Liverpool?"

The waiter returned with two pint glasses and a small bowl of mixed nuts.

Emily reached out with her glass to touch Fiona's in a toast. "Here's to your return to Paris, and hopefully the first trip of many. I'd love to show you more of my favorite areas."

Fiona was struck again by how green Emily's eyes were. "I'd love that. It's obvious you know Paris very well."

"Where are you staying?" Emily reached for a handful of nuts.

"I'm on the Right Bank, just north of the Marais, at a small place called the Hotel Beaumarchais."

"That's a great area. Lots of the new chefs have opened restaurants in that neighborhood. Maybe we could wander around over there next time and try one of those." She took another handful of nuts. "These aren't doing it for me.

Are you hungry?"

As if in response, Fiona's stomach growled, and they both laughed. "Apparently."

Emily signaled the waiter for menus, and they spent a couple of minutes browsing through.

"I think I'll have *steak frites*," Fiona said. "I'm pretty sure that's what I smelled when we first arrived."

"It's very good. I think I'll have the fish special. The fish is so much better here than at home."

"Better than fish and chips? That's one of my favorite meals at the pub."

"That is *not* the kind of fish I meant." Emily said in mock disapproval then smiled, adding, "Nothing can beat a good fish and chips."

"I agree."

The conversation flowed from one topic to the next—from food, to travel, to movies they liked. Fiona felt comfortably full and just a little bit buzzed from the second beer. "That steak was absolutely delicious. Thank you for telling me to order it medium rare. I'd never have dared to do that on my own."

"Trust me—you would *not* want to see the waiter's expression if you'd asked for his beautiful steak well done!" They both laughed.

"Have you lived in Oxford long?"

"Just since I went to attend University. I'm originally from Cornwall. How about you? How long have you been in Liverpool?"

"My whole life. I oversee the sales team at my family's window blinds company. Not a very exciting job, I'm afraid."

"I'm sure your parents are thrilled."

"Actually, my father died a few years ago, and my brother, Kevin, is running it now." Fiona paused, her throat tightening. "And I lost my Mum a month ago." She took a quick sip of coffee around the lump in her throat.

Emily reached over to touch her arm. "I am so sorry. Both of my parents are gone, too. They died in a car accident years ago, but I still miss them. Do you mind if I ask what happened?"

"Complications from the flu. If I'm honest, it was a blessing. She'd been suffering from Alzheimer's, and she had more bad days than good these last few months." Fiona had to clear her throat to continue. "She wasn't always easy to live with, but she was an important person in my life."

They lapsed into silence, gazing out at the street, each lost in her own thoughts as they sipped their coffee.

When Fiona turned to face Emily, the sympathy and warmth in her eyes made her blurt out, "What am I going to do without her? And what am I going to do with the rest of my life?" She stopped, embarrassed at her own outburst. She held her napkin to her mouth, taking a deep breath to hold back her tears.

Emily took her other hand, squeezing it. "You've had a rough few months. It can't have been easy."

Fiona instinctively pulled her hand away— desperately trying to hang onto what little self-control she had left. "Thank you." She fumbled with her backpack, afraid to meet Emily's eyes again. "Um... I'm sorry, but I have a splitting headache. I'm going to head back to my hotel."

"Please don't apologize. I understand."

"Thank you so much for the tour and this delicious dinner. How much do I owe you?" she pulled out two twenty-euro notes.

Emily motioned them away. "Please, it's my treat. You can buy next time."

Fiona started to argue, but her control was crumbling.

She needed to escape before she lost it completely. With another mumbled thanks, she set off blindly toward the noise and activity of the large boulevard. One block up she saw the large "M" indicating a metro stop. The map at the entrance helped her figure out how to get back to her hotel.

Twenty minutes later, she opened the door to her room and fell on the bed sobbing. She realized dimly it was the first time she'd broken down since her mother had died. She'd been numb that first night when she'd heard from the nursing home, then she'd had to stay strong for her brother and the employees at the factory through all the funeral arrangements. She hadn't even cried at the service itself. It had all felt slightly unreal.

Tonight, Emily's concern had seemed truly heartfelt. It was the first time Fiona had felt someone understood her anguish, her enormous sense of loss. It was not something she could share with anyone at work, and her best friend, Nena, had been away for a couple months in Ireland taking care of her own mother.

She let herself sob until she felt wrung out and had no tears left. She wept for her Mum's lost years to Alzheimer's, and for the life her mother might have had under different circumstances.

One thing was suddenly very clear to Fiona. She did not want to let that happen to her.

Chapter 8

Jane blinked as she came out of the dark theater and into the bright sun. When she'd seen the listing for *Casablanca* the day before, she'd decided that this morning she would make the trip over to catch the early matinee showing. It was still one of her all-time favorite movies. Classic love story, the girl in love with one man but married to another, throw in a little war intrigue, and some scary bad guys, and it kept you on the edge of your seat every time.

Since she was going down memory lane, she decided she would also go see if Francois' family bakery was still in business. She could then grab a bite to eat somewhere nearby before heading at 4:00 to meet Fiona, who'd texted saying she'd found an interesting exhibit at a museum called the Jacquemart Andre.

On the bus, she glanced through her email, noticing there were none from Jack. She couldn't decide if she was relieved or disappointed. She had asked him to not contact her, but she'd assumed he wouldn't be able to resist.

She wouldn't think about that. She'd think instead about how much fun it would be if the bakery were still there and even better if Francois' family still owned it. The Sunday dinners with him and his large family—and the lively discussions of everything from politics to the arts—had enriched her life so much more than anything she'd learned in her formal classes.

She stepped off the bus and couldn't believe how little the neighborhood had changed. The small grocery on the corner had been replaced by a cell phone store, but otherwise it looked exactly as she remembered it. She took a deep breath and set off.

As she approached the end of the block, she was afraid to look, but there it was, *Ma Petite Choux*, the affectionate term Francois' father had used for his wife.

Jane paused across the street, her heart beating fast. The glass display case in the window looked the same and was filled with beautiful pastries, and there was also a new plaque next to the door— 'Best Croissant in 2017'. Jane's mouth watered suddenly, remembering his father's amazing *pains au chocolat* croissants.

She walked across the street and through the open door and was immediately enveloped by the warm, yeasty smell that brought memories flooding back. She breathed deeply.

"*Bonjour, Madame,*" The woman behind the counter looked to be in her early twenties, with short hair died a bright red.

"*Bonjour,*" Jane replied. "*Un pain au chocolat,* please." Could this be a niece, perhaps? She saw no sign of Francois' mother or father.

"Anything else?"

"No, *merci beaucoup.*"

"Two euros please."

"*Excusez-moi,* but does the Mercier family still own

this bakery?"

"Oh, no, Madame. My parents bought it in 2005."

Jane tried to swallow her disappointment. "Do you know anything about where they might be these days?"

The young woman shrugged a class Gallic shrug and strolled to the back, where Jane could hear a rapid-fire conversation. She soon returned, shaking her head. "No, Maman has not stayed in touch with them, but she said the son stops by occasionally."

Jane ripped a page from her notebook and hastily scribbled her name, phone number and email address. "Would you please give this to him if you see him? I would really appreciate it."

The young woman glanced down at the paper with little change to her expression, and nodded, tucking it into her jeans pocket. "Have a nice day, *Madame*," the young woman said, glancing pointedly behind Jane at the next customer.

"*Merci beaucoup.*" Jane exited and hesitated a moment before turning left toward what she hoped would still be a small park. She was relieved to find it still there, and she sat on one of its stone benches, pulling out the *pain au chocolat* and taking a large bite. She sighed. Another disappointment.

"Looking for the second piece of chocolate?" a teasing voice said into her ear, and with a yelp, she turned to meet Francois' dancing eyes.

"*Toi?* What are you doing here?" Jane spluttered, trying not to choke on the bite she'd taken.

Francois came around to the front of the bench and pulled her into a hug. "Me? What are *you* doing here?"

She started to speak, but he held up his hand. "This conversation will take more than a few minutes. Have you had lunch?" She shook her head. "*Bon.* Come join me and tell me why you're in Paris, and what you've been doing for the last thirty years." His grin hadn't changed at all, though his eyes were now surrounded by fine wrinkles and stylish designer glasses. She noticed as she followed him that he'd also put on a little bit of weight, but it suited him.

They were soon seated, champagne bubbling merrily in front of them. Francois raised his. "To chance meetings."

They clinked glasses, and Jane smiled. "I can't believe it. It feels like I conjured you up by taking a bite of my croissant."

"Not as good as my father's, was it?"

"Definitely not. Why does no one else put in a second piece of chocolate?"

"I don't know. They should."

"She said your family sold it in 2005?"

"Yes. As you know, my father always wanted me to take it over, but I never loved the actual baking like he did, so I went on to business school instead and helped with the accounts until my father retired."

The waiter arrived to take their orders. "It sounds like you've kept up with your French," Francois said, reaching for his champagne to take a sip.

"Thank you for saying that, but it still feels really rusty." Jane noticed he wasn't wearing a wedding ring, though she could see the faded evidence of one.

"Let's start with the obvious," Francois said. "What are you doing in Paris?"

"I guess you'd say I'm taking an unexpected leave of absence from my life in Boston."

Francois glanced toward where she was twisting her own wedding ring nervously, his eyebrows raised.

"I'm not ready to talk about it yet."

"Okay." He gave her an appraising look. "You know you look just the same. How do you manage that?"

Jane blushed. "Francois, I do *not* look the same, but thank you for saying so."

"You're still beautiful," he said softly. After a moment, he continued. "If you don't want to talk about that, tell me what you've done for the last thirty years. I know you're married. Do you have children?"

"I have one daughter, Kallie. She's just graduated from college and gotten her first job in New York city. Hard to believe she's older than we were when we knew each other. What about you?"

"I have two daughters, one who's twenty and one who's twenty-three."

"Do they live in Paris with you?"

"Actually, I don't live in Paris. After we got married, Sandrine and I moved to Rennes, and my children live there. Do you know it?"

"No."

"It's about ninety minutes away on the TGV—the fast train."

"Is your job in Rennes?"

"Only partly. I work for a small grocery store chain and part of my job is visiting our various locations, so I'm on the road a lot."

Jane choked, and put down her fork and knife with a clatter. "You don't work for Bon Gout by any chance?"

Francois looked surprised and pleased. "Yes, in fact, exactly. How do you know Bon Gout?"

"Small world! I took a cooking class earlier this week and one of the women I partnered with works there. Véronique Moreau."

"Véronique? She's one of our rising stars."

"I really like her. I'm having dinner at her house tonight with Fiona Braxton, the other woman I met in the class."

"What a small world indeed."

"What do you do at Bon Gout?"

"I oversee all the baked goods we offer, so I travel to the various stores and to the commercial bakeries that distribute to the stores."

The waiter cleared their dishes, then brought coffee.

Francois' look was intense. "I always thought you would come back to Paris," he said, swirling his coffee.

"So did I." Jane held his gaze for a moment. "But then I met Jack."

"Doesn't Jack like to travel?"

"Not unless it's New Hampshire, or it involves golf," Jane said bitterly. "Sorry. It's a particularly sensitive subject right now. Does your wife like to travel?"

Francois shook his head. "No, Sandrine never felt she could take the time away from her law practice. It's one of the reasons we got a divorce."

"That's Jack, too. There's always some deal that needs him to stay close to home." She took a sip, before adding, "I really thought with Kallie heading off he'd feel differently." She shook her head in frustration.

They were both silent, then when Francois spoke, Jane could hear the sadness in his voice. "Choosing to stay together or to separate is not an easy decision."

"No, it isn't." She took a deep breath. "Do you regret the decision you made?"

"Sometimes, but I realized she was never going to change. When we first got married, I didn't mind it. She was the ambitious one, the driven one. She tried to be involved with the girls and their activities, but her first priority was always making law partner. When the girls left for university, we lost the only conversation topic we'd shared for years. We didn't even know each other anymore. Is that what happened to you?"

"No, I was blindsided, to be honest."

"Did this just happen when Kallie left?"

"Yes."

"Now do you want to talk about it?" His voice was gentle.

She realized suddenly she did, and nodded slowly. "I had planned a romantic evening sketching out all the fun trips Jack and I would take, but instead Jack announced he'd bought land in New Hampshire to build a forever home. Surprisingly, that was not on *my* list of destinations." Jane smiled wryly.

Francois laughed out loud. "Why does that not surprise me?"

Jane sobered. "But that turned out to just be the first bombshell. He ended the conversation saying maybe we should 'rethink' everything. That maybe we should get a divorce. I did *not* see that coming."

"Jane, I am so sorry."

Jane looked at Francois, her face distraught. "I felt *so* betrayed. This was the man I'd given my heart to. And my trust. I thought we shared everything. I suddenly felt like I didn't even know him. How could he buy land without even asking me? Had we really drifted that far apart? He said he'd been trying to talk to me about it, but I don't think I'm *that* oblivious."

"For us, we were drifting apart for years, so when we finally talked about it, there was sadness, but no anger. It felt like a foregone conclusion."

"Oh, there was definitely anger in my case. Once I got over the initial shock, I just got more and more angry. That night I lay tossing and turning in one of the guest bedrooms, trying to figure out where and when things had started to go sideways, and by the next morning I couldn't even look at him. I left and stayed with my best friend, Angela until I could find a flight out of there."

"So, you never came up with any evidence of what might have happened?"

"No, we've always had plenty of things we do on our own, so there was no change there, and he didn't seem any different. Not distant or cold. Nothing like that. I know I've been distracted and sad recently with Kallie packing to leave, but this came out of nowhere." Jane twisted the ring on her finger again angrily. "Angela was convinced there must be more to it so she has started digging around on social media and last night sent me pictures of him at some recent work events. He does look *awfully* friendly with his office manager, Barbara, so maybe she's right. I just don't know anymore."

Francois sighed. "It's good you got away from Boston to give yourself some space and time to work through it all and figure out what *you* want."

"Thank you for letting me vent." Jane reached across to squeeze his hand. "I'm so glad I ran into you today."

"I'm here if you need a shoulder to cry on, or a sympathetic ear." He reached for his phone. "Let me send you all my contact info. I don't want to lose touch again."

"And here's mine." She paused. "You're the first person I've talked to about this besides Angela. It's still so raw. But when you told me about you and Sandrine, I felt safe sharing it."

"I'm glad you did." Francois' phone buzzed and he reluctantly signaled for the check. "I'm sorry, but I have to get going or I'll miss my train."

"Me, too. I'm meeting a friend at the Jacquemart Andre."

"I love that museum. You can let me know how you like it next time we see each other." Francois smiled and he gave her a tight hug. "And I hope that's soon."

Chapter 9

"Véronique?"

She looked up, distracted.

David was perched on the edge of her desk and wagged his finger at her accusingly. "I thought you were going to stop by. I want to show you my ideas for the website for the London store. Didn't you see my text?"

"Sorry. Claude and his team are on my back again about the London delivery schedules." She glanced at her phone and saw it was 1:30, and as if in recognition, her stomach growled loudly."

"I take you haven't had lunch, either?"

She shook her head.

David stood and came around to peer at her computer over her shoulder. "That doesn't look like a delivery schedule," he said drily.

Véronique looked sheepish, "You know I hate that stuff. I might have been distracting myself by designing the window displays instead."

He laughed and studied her screen for a moment. "These look great. See how much fun the creative side is?"

"You don't have to tell me. That's my favorite part."

"Mine, too. I'd much rather spend less time on the technical aspects and making the websites functional, but it's a necessary evil. Speaking of which..."

"Website design for London. Right. Okay, lead the way."

Véronique rose and followed David to his desk, where he pulled out two large story boards. They spent the next few minutes comparing them, and David made a few quick changes with a black sharpie. "Okay, now I feel like I have a good idea which way to go," he said finally. "Let's go get something to eat."

They made their way to *Le Mistral*, a small restaurant around the corner that was the regular hangout for many of the offices in the area. It was starting to empty as the lunch crowd headed back to work and they were quickly seated at a corner table. There was one large table near the bar that was still occupied, and she noticed with a shock that Jean-Pierre was seated on the far side. Her annoyance at his hesitation on the phone earlier about getting off at a decent hour came flooding back.

He was gesticulating as he told them a story and she took advantage of his distraction to watch him. One lock of his brown hair had fallen across his eyebrow, giving him almost a professorial air, and his wire-rimmed glasses completed the impression. His dark slacks and tailored linen shirt emphasized his slim build. *He really is so handsome*, she thought, feeling her annoyance disappearing to be replaced by a tug of desire. How long had it been since they'd had a leisurely romantic weekend together? She made a quick promise to herself she'd make them get away as soon as she got through this store opening in London and he finished his big pitch.

At that moment, Jean-Pierre glanced around and with a surprised exclamation, he jumped up and came over, giving Véronique a warm kiss and David a firm handshake. She could smell wine and coffee on his breath.

"What are you doing here?" David asked. "I thought you were chained to your desk, working on your pitch for the marketing contract for Vitesse."

"We just finished the final draft, so we decided to get something to eat and let our minds have a break before we head back to do our final practice this afternoon." He looked sheepishly at Véronique. "I was going to text you to join us but figured you'd be bored with all the shop talk." He glanced at his watch. "You guys are also eating late."

"Yes, we're buried too," she said, but then added, "You do remember that Jane and Fiona are coming over for dinner tonight, right?"

"Yes, of course. That should be fine. The practice won't take too long." He spoke with confidence but Véronique had her doubts.

"Okay...."

David spoke up. "Since I have you both here, I want to confirm you *are* coming to Mathilde's birthday party this weekend, right? Annette has been complaining that we haven't seen you two in forever and she will be very disappointed if you don't show."

"We'll be there," Jean-Pierre said, grinning. "It'll be great to see all three of you. Let's also look at our calendars when we're there to plan a grown-up dinner. It really has been way too long."

"It has been. With our crazy work schedules, and now all of Mathilde's activities, I feel like we don't have a minute to even breathe, much less have a leisurely meal. We'll plan it for *after* the London opening, right, Véronique?"

"Yes, please. Though it will be a minor miracle if we manage to find a day that works for all four of us, plus find a babysitter." They all laughed, and Jean-Pierre rose to return to the table with his team.

"Don't forget about tonight, Jean-Pierre." He waved his acknowledgement as he turned away. "I'll believe it when I see it," Véronique said under her breath.

David raised his wine glass. "Look at the positive. If he gets home late, you'll have a fun girls night."

"Good point."

"Another good thing. You only have two more weeks to fret about your opening, then it'll be over and you'll be celebrating your shining success."

"Don't jinx it. Let's talk about something else. How are *you* doing?"

"I'm buried. Besides your site, we're revamping the ones for the stores in the south and trying to come up with a new email campaign. And Camille took advantage of our fifteen-minute walk to our cars the other night to tell me all the things I need to do for her team and that she needs to be my first priority."

"She's a piece of work," Véronique said sarcastically.

"I know you're not a fan, but things seem worse lately. What's up between you two?"

"She keeps sniping at me behind my back on this project trying to make me look bad. I think she's jealous of all the attention I'm getting from the big bosses."

"C'mon, are you sure you're not being overly paranoid?"

"I'm sure. Your problem is you always think the best of everyone."

"I wouldn't go that far. Is there something else?"

"Why do you ask?"

"I don't know. You just seem more on edge. Sometimes you fly off the handle over dumb stuff. It's not like you."

"You're right." Véronique glanced quickly over to where Jean-Pierre and his team were rising to head out and lowered her voice. "There *is* something else. I'm very frustrated with Jean-Pierre. We had a huge fight the other night, and we've been bickering ever since."

"About what?"

"What do you think? About when we should start a family."

"Ah, yeah that's a tough subject."

"We'd been saying we'd start when we turned thirty but we've both got way too much going on right now. For me, the opening of the London store, and for him, that Vitesse pitch and a couple of other contracts. We can't possibly add a baby to the mix."

"I think you're right, but I'll also say, from my experience, there's never a perfect time. There will always be stuff going on at work."

"I know that's true. But it really feels like we are both at a critical moment in our careers. Him with his pitch to Vitesse and the London opening for me. I can't mess this up. Plus arguing about it is exhausting. We're going around in circles, and he won't let it go." Véronique gulped her wine. "You know very well that trying to coerce me into agreeing to *anything* is not a good strategy."

David grinned. "I definitely know that."

"I've learned so much setting up this store. It's my chance to prove myself. To the leadership team, but also to myself."

"I get it. It's the first time you've had the added responsibility of overseeing everything so it's your stepping stone for future opportunities." He paused and squeezed her hand. "And you're doing a great job. You should be proud of yourself. I've worked on other store openings, and you've handled it better than most. You're such a consummate professional. You make everyone feel like they're contributing. You obviously have a plan in mind and know what you need to do to achieve that plan."

"Thank you. That means a lot."

"And on the baby question, I can tell you that with Mathilde it completely changed our life and our priorities."

"That's what I keep telling him."

"You're at a crucial point in your career. The big bosses love you, but that can change in a heartbeat. Tell Jean-Pierre to chill out."

"Thank you. I will."

"I can ask Mathilde to be extra whiny and needy at her birthday party."

Véronique laughed. "No, that's okay. Thank you. This has really helped. Okay, let's get the check and get out of here. I've still got a couple more things to do, and I've got guests coming, remember?"

"Oh, that's right." David signaled the waiter, and Véronique's phone pinged. She opened the email, then cursed under her breath.

"What's up?"

"Speak of the devil. Camille just sent an email to the President, copying me, asking to see my inventory list for London because 'she is sure I have been thorough and she can learn from me.' Yeah, right. She's hoping I don't have one." Véronique grabbed her purse. "But I do, and I need to send it pronto. That bitch. How much do I owe?"

"This one's on me. You can pay when the four of us go out for our grown-up dinner."

"No way, I'm not falling for that. I'll get lunch next time."

David grinned. "Deal. Good luck with everything tonight."

"Thank you for everything. For getting me out of the office. For buying lunch. And mostly for always just being there."

Chapter 10

Jane and Fiona emerged from the Abbesses metro stop and found themselves in the middle of a boisterous flea market.

Jane looked back at Fiona with a wide grin. "I would have suggested leaving the museum a bit earlier if I'd known this was here. Can we find a treasure or two in thirty minutes?"

In front of them stood a woman selling silver flatware and lace tablecloths, runners, and napkins; next to her stood a grey-haired man selling crockery, from small pitchers to teapots to casserole dishes. Next over on the row were racks of vintage clothing, and boxes of old books and records. And everywhere were throngs of people.

"Let's give it a try," Fiona said. "I'll start over there at those old books."

"I want to look at the silverware and tablecloths. Meet you back here?"

Twenty-nine minutes later, Jane arrived back, slightly breathless, and Fiona smiled and held up a black bag. Both turned at the sound of Véronique's voice.

"*Bonsoir*, Jane, Fiona." She embraced them both warmly. "I am so glad to see you both again. I forgot the flea market would be here today. What a crowd. Did you have a chance to look around at all?"

"Not only look around, but find treasures, right Fiona?" Jane held up her bag with a grin.

Véronique linked her arms through theirs. "*Bon!* I'm glad." As they made their way up the street, she added, "Jean-Pierre has been held up for a bit. This big pitch his office is doing."

"Oh no." Jane glanced over, seeing Véronique's grimace.

Véronique shrugged. "*C'est la vie*. When I heard they were doing the final practice tonight, I knew it might happen and told myself right then I would not let it ruin our evening."

"Good for you," Fiona said. "I'm glad we could get together again, whether we meet him or not."

They passed through a large, gray double door into a courtyard and Véronique sounded sheepish as she said, "I'm sorry, but we don't have an elevator, so we'll have to walk up the three flights. I hope that is okay."

"No problem. I need the exercise with all the bread and jam I've been eating," Fiona said cheerfully.

They emerged slightly breathless onto a small landing and Véronique ushered them into a bright living room, the setting sun blazing through the far window. The space was larger than Jane had expected, with bright red kitchen cabinetry and appliances along the far wall. Next to the kitchen, they could see a small round table, set with four places. A low leather couch, and a plush, printed fabric chair flanked a glass coffee table, which held an ice bucket, champagne flutes, and two ceramic plates filled with delicious-looking appetizers. The room was simple but elegant.

"This is adorable, Véronique."

"*Merci.*" Véronique blushed with obvious pleasure.

Once they were seated, Véronique lifted out the dripping bottle from the ice bucket. "*Champagne?*"

"Yes, please," Jane and Fiona said simultaneously, and they all laughed.

"I've always wondered why at home we only drink champagne for special occasions," Jane said. *And here it's the second time today, though lunch with Francois feels like a lifetime ago. I could get used to this lifestyle,* she thought with a small smile.

"Jean-Pierre and I often serve it like this, with canapés. Is that the right word?"

"I'd probably call them appetizers. What about you, Fiona?"

"I call them canapés, like Véronique. Or sometimes I'll just say nibbles if it's more casual."

"That's a fun word. With friends, I'd say finger food."

"Wait." Véronique looked panicked. "I should write all of these names down."

"Don't worry. Whatever you call them, they look great, Véronique."

Jane reached down next to her and pulled out the books she'd bought and giftwrapped. "These are to say thank you for inviting us tonight," she said as she handed them to Véronique.

"You didn't need to do that," Véronique said, but she eagerly unwrapped them. "These look wonderful! I'm always looking for a good book or website for the names of cheeses so now I will have them at my fingertips whenever I need them. And Jean-Pierre will love this other one on wine pairings. Thank you so much." She stood and came over to give Jane a hug, then refilled their glasses. "And what about the flea market? What did you find there?"

Jane reached into her bag again and pulled out a lace tablecloth which she gently unfolded.

"That's beautiful," Fiona breathed.

"It's just like one my grandmother had. She lived just outside of Boston, so when I moved there after college, we'd cook together for Sunday dinners. She's the one who taught me my first recipe when I was about six."

"That's a wonderful story," Fiona said. "I never knew my grandmother."

"I have a notebook at home full of her recipes." Jane paused, then added quietly, "She died the same year my daughter, Kallie, was born."

"I'm sorry they didn't have the chance to get to know one another." Véronique said quietly, then handed the tablecloth back and squeezed Jane's hand.

Jane placed it carefully back into her bag then turned to Fiona. "What did you find?"

"I bought a piece of clothing."

"Fun! Will you model it for us?"

Fiona carried her bag around the corner, and when she reappeared, Jane clapped loudly. "*Très chic!*"

Fiona did a slow turn before striking a modelling pose and giggling nervously. The black leather coat hugged her body in a smooth unbroken line from neckline to mid-thigh. The front zipper was offset and zipped upward at an angle. When she unzipped it, it formed a wide lapel across her shoulders. She was smiling broadly. "I couldn't believe it fit me. I've never seen anything like it."

"Maybe it's from one of the fashion shows? Did the seller say anything?"

"He claimed it was a designer piece, but I don't care

either way. I've never owned anything like this. I love it."

"It fits like a glove," exclaimed Jane, but then with a mock frown, added, "But now I won't be able to find you in a crowd. You'll be in black like all the other Parisians."

They all laughed as Fiona carefully put it away.

Véronique rose. "I think it's time to eat. Jean-Pierre will just have to eat the leftovers." She looked slightly annoyed as she pulled out the lasagna.

"Véronique, what can we do to help?"

"Could you slice the baguette, Fiona? And Jane, can you pour each of us a glass of wine from the bottle on the table? It's from Vézelay, which is where I'm from."

"Where is Vézelay?"

"In Bourgogne, just a couple of hours south of Paris."

"Is that where you met Jean-Pierre?"

"No, my friend Marie-Claire introduced us here in Paris. She knew Jean-Pierre's brother and they threw a party for some of us when I graduated. A lot of our friends ended up in Paris because there are so many jobs here."

"I assume it's expensive, though, right?"

"Definitely. So generally people start by living in the center of the city, then move to the suburbs when they have children."

"Do you think you two will have children? I'm sorry if that's too personal." Jane asked as she took a sip of wine. "This is delicious, by the way."

Véronique brought the steaming dish over and motioned for them both to sit down. When they were settled, she said, "Yes, we do want to have children someday, but we're having a huge argument about when. He can't understand why I'm not quite ready."

"Ah, the age-old problem of men thinking they should make our decisions for us. Fiona and I were just talking about that at the museum this afternoon."

"To be fair, we did say we'd start at thirty, but both of us are at critical points in our careers right now, so I think it makes sense to wait a bit longer. He disagrees."

"That sounds logical to me."

"He seems to think we can add a baby into the mix and things will go along just as they always have. It's very frustrating." Véronique's face was flushed, and Jane could see how stressed she was. She then shook her head. "I admit the whole idea of babies is frankly overwhelming right now. When I try to imagine all the changes that would have to happen, I don't see how anyone manages to balance it all. Jane, how did you do it?"

"When I had Kallie, I moved into a less demanding job but at the same company and that gave me more flexibility. I don't know if that's an option, or even of interest to you, but that was what worked for me."

"I've been with Bon Gout for five years and really like it so I do want to stay. I guess I'll just figure it out when it happens."

"In my opinion, it needs to be a decision you and Jean-Pierre reach together. You need to make him understand your priorities and your reasons for waiting." She paused. "Talking through what you want in your marriage and in your life is the most important thing there is for a healthy marriage." She added bitterly, "I just learned that the hard way."

At their questioning looks, Jane continued in an unsteady voice. "I'm not in Paris on vacation. I'm here because out of the blue, my husband of twenty-three years told me he thought we should get a divorce."

"*Mon Dieu*," Véronique murmured.

There was a long moment of stunned silence.

"What happened?" Fiona asked in a whisper.

"Jack and I didn't have that heart-to-heart talk about our personal priorities until it was too late." She took a large gulp of her wine. "In the early days of our marriage, we didn't have much vacation time or extra money, and we were taking care of Jack's aging parents, so if we did go away, it was always within a three-hour drive. That made perfect sense, but as the years passed, I would try to suggest trips further away and Jack always shut me down. He had legitimate reasons: something at work; or some sort of family obligation. So, I didn't push it. I didn't argue, but I assumed that at some point, we would have more flexibility and I would get to plan the trips I'd put off for so long. It turned out that staying close to home wasn't just a short-term preference for him. It was all he was *ever* interested in.

"Looking back, I should have asked more questions, but I acquiesced because I always thought I'd have my turn when Kallie was gone. What I didn't tell you is on our honeymoon, we wrote up a list of places to visit one day and I kept it all these years. I thought it was an actual plan, but he didn't even remember us doing it. That's why, in my mind, he broke that plan. Turns out I was just being naïve."

"Jane, you weren't being naïve," Véronique said. "How could you have known that he didn't feel the same way you did about the paper?"

"I guess that's true, but what it also made me realize was that over all those years, it never even occurred to him to *ask me* if I might want something different. That he never saw what *I* was giving up by *not* traveling. It made me feel he'd never really known me, and that's what hurt the most."

Véronique cleared the dishes and Jane stood and opened another bottle and refilled everyone's glasses.

"What are you going to do?" Fiona asked in a hushed tone.

"I honestly don't know, but I do feel better having shared it with you two." As she sat down again, various thoughts and emotions that had been percolating in the back of her mind began to coalesce into an idea.

It had started her first morning with her arrival at the apartment, when she'd felt overwhelmingly that she was back where she belonged. Then at the cooking class, she'd been filled with joy and a sense of accomplishment as she learned the various recipes and reveled in being once more in a well-equipped kitchen. Another piece of the puzzle had then clicked into place with her conversation with Francois, and the realization, for better or worse, that she might very well end up getting divorced.

"I want to sign up for a professional cooking course," Jane blurted out, not quite believing she'd said it out loud.

Fiona spluttered. "Where did that come from?"

"You asked what I'm going to do now, and it suddenly came to me. For the first time in my adult life, I have no set agenda and no one to worry about or take care of. Maybe it's time to take care of myself." She stopped suddenly, overwhelmed by a mix of emotions. Excitement, but also sadness. And anger. And regret.

Véronique and Fiona both looked at her in questioning silence, waiting for her to continue.

She forced a smile. "Maybe I can turn what feels like a disastrous life change into a positive one. Maybe there is a silver lining to this black cloud. Am I completely nuts?"

"*Non*, I think it is a wonderful idea." Véronique said, looking thoughtful. "I have worked with chefs from some of the professional schools who teach classes at our stores. I would be happy to send an email on your behalf to the two I know—the *Ecole Langelier* and *La Cuisine Française*. Jane, you do realize those classes are usually in French with an English translator, right? Are you comfortable with that?"

"I think so. My French is coming back, though I'm sure I'll need to learn a lot of new vocabulary."

"I can give you the names of a couple of good reference books for that, but first and foremost, you need to go online tomorrow morning and actually apply. I can then send the emails to introduce you. After that, all we can do is—how do you say it—cross our fingers?"

"Thank you, Véronique. That sounds like a good plan."

"Jane, this would be a huge decision," Fiona looked worried.

"She's right. These courses last for several months," added Véronique. "What about your job at home?"

"That's a great question. I've been unhappy for a while, so I'd already been toying with the idea of quitting, but I don't know. I still can't believe I'm even considering this, but now that we're talking about it, I do want to see it through and at least get an application in. I still have to get accepted, so we'll see what happens."

"Promise me you'll really think it all through before you commit to anything." Fiona said, still looking worried. "I know it has nothing to do with me, really, and I don't even know you that well, but I just don't want you leaping into something you'll regret."

Jane felt deeply touched by Fiona's concern. "Thank you. I promise." She paused before adding, "I can't believe I'm actually going to do this."

"You are a brave woman, Jane, to take such a leap," Véronique said. "We are here to support you." They all raised their glasses.

Jane turned to Fiona. "Speaking of support, Fiona, we haven't talked about your situation. I'm sorry it's been all about me. I want to say again how sorry I am for your loss."

"Thank you. It is going to be hard to go back and pick up the pieces of my life again. I've been so focused on taking care of Mum."

"Maybe for you, like for me, it's time to focus on yourself," Jane said with a sad smile.

"I think you may be right. I feel like this trip has been the first step in that journey. It's given me new confidence in myself."

"You can give us an update at the end of the month," Véronique piped up. "You *are* planning to come to my store opening, right?"

"Absolutely. Visiting London more often is already one of my goals and it gives me the perfect incentive to put that plan into action."

They raised their glasses again, and Véronique rose. "I bought us a fruit tart from my favorite bakery for dessert. Does anyone want coffee or tea?"

Just then, they heard the sound of the lock turning, and Jean-Pierre walked in, smiling and apologizing. "I am so sorry to be so late." He came over to shake their hands, then went to where Véronique was filling the kettle and hugged her to him, murmuring something into her ear.

Véronique pushed him away after a moment, laughing. "Jean-Pierre, you crazy man," but she was smiling up at him, and Jane felt a quick twinge of envy. She and Jack had looked at each other like that once upon a time.

Jane and Fiona stayed just long enough to be polite, and when Jane got home, she opened her computer to look up the two cooking schools. Her quick glance showed that each had new programs starting soon and her heart quickened. If she chose to pursue it, would Jack understand? Or was that choice, in effect, also a choice to end her marriage?

Chapter 11

The next morning, Fiona felt her phone vibrate and pulling it out, squinted at the screen. "Next time I think it's a brilliant idea to drink so much wine with dinner, after sharing a bottle of champagne with canapes, please talk me out of it."

"It was good wine; you have to admit," Jane replied, her voice slightly hoarse.

Fiona groaned. "It was, but my stomach is not happy this morning."

"I won't deny we might have overdone it a wee bit. I'm sitting in Sylvie's café right now with a cup of her special hangover remedy."

"I'm praying for my paracetamol to start working."

"This will probably sound like a crazy idea, based on how we feel, but I found a champagne tasting at a wine store near me that says it's focused on small producers, and you went on and on last night about how you'd never tasted champagne you liked before. I'd love to know more about the small producers and at a tasting, we wouldn't be drinking large quantities, right? How about it?"

"Maybe. What time?"

"It's at 6:00. You could meet me here any time after 5:00, and we could walk over."

"It depends how I'm feeling at that point. There was a note under my door when I got home last night about a walking tour of the Marais that's included in my package. I think the fresh air and exercise will feel good. Do you want to come?"

"I don't think so, thanks. I need to get these school applications filled out, and I want to take my time and do it right. Let's check in later. Maybe I'll reach out to Véronique to see if she wants to join us for dinner. Something casual."

"Good idea. Okay. Bye."

Fiona sat for a moment after she hung up, letting the medicine work its magic, then headed out. On the elevator ride down, her thoughts turned to Emily briefly, as they had done several times over the last twenty-four hours, and she berated herself again for running off so abruptly. Pushing through the door to the reception area, she glanced up and stopped dead, her heart pounding.

Emily rose from the small seating area. "Hello, and surprise?" She hesitated slightly before adding, "I wondered if you'd be interested in getting a coffee?"

"Uh, sure." Fiona led the way across the street and when they'd given their orders, Fiona turned. "How in the world did you find me?"

"I remembered the name of your hotel from our chat. I hope you don't mind," Emily added quickly, looking much less sure of herself.

"I don't mind at all. I'm very glad you did." Fiona took a sip of her *café crème* and grimaced slightly.

"Are you okay?"

Fiona rubbed her head. "Yes, nothing serious. Just a little overindulgence last night with my friends from the cooking class."

"Ah."

"I enjoyed showing you my favorite little corner of Paris."

"I enjoyed it too. And the dinner afterward." Fiona took another sip of coffee. "I'm sorry I left so abruptly."

"That's okay."

"It's not okay. It was ridiculous."

"You've just lost your mother. I completely understand you're having a hard time with that. I hope it wasn't something I said?"

"Just the opposite. You were so kind. It was actually the first time that it really hit me. I've been so busy trying to be strong for everyone."

"I really do know how it feels. Even though it's been years, I still have moments when I just want to be able to call my mum and tell her some funny story."

Fiona nodded. "I've had moments like that already on this trip."

The sun was warm overhead, and Fiona felt herself relax. "I'm supposed to be going on a tour this morning of the Marais. Do you want to join me?"

"What are you supposed to see?"

Fiona scrolled through her phone. "The tour is called 'Life in the 19th Century' and includes the Cognacq-Jay Museum and then Victor Hugo's house."

"Emily?" A quiet voice with a French accent spoke behind them suddenly. They both turned.

"*Béatrice? Mais qu'est-ce que tu fais là?* What are you doing here?" Emily jumped up to greet a woman seated two rows behind them, giving her a huge hug, then leading her back to meet Fiona. She was small, with pixie-like features and beautiful dark hair that was cut short. She had dark brown eyes and a small dimple in one cheek. Her jacket was a deep forest green, and she wore it over a black turtleneck. Her designer jeans ended with folded cuffs above a pair of sleek black pumps. Fiona immediately felt dowdy and awkward.

"Fiona, this is a dear friend of mine, Béatrice Simon. We taught together at the Sorbonne when I was here for a one-year exchange." She and Béatrice exchanged a look and Fiona felt a small shock. They had been more than just friends.

"Do you have time to join us for a coffee?" Emily asked and without hesitation Béatrice returned to her own table to gather her belongings. Fiona had a moment of déjà vu from when she and Emily had met.

After Béatrice was settled and had ordered, Emily asked, "How funny to run into you here."

"I'm pulling information together for a class I'll teach in September called the History of Retail so I'm spending time at the Cognacq-Jay Museum. It's not far from here so I've become a bit of a regular at this café because it has great food. What about you? What are you doing here?"

"I'm in Paris working on a paper on Notre Dame and Fiona and I met by chance over near there. We were just talking about the Cognacq-Jay, in fact, because the folks from her package tour are headed there this morning. Do you want to join us?"

"I'll walk down there with you, though I'm sure I know more than your tour guide, Fiona."

What a snob! Fiona's initial discomfort changed to dislike. She forced a smile.

"How big is the group?"

"I'm not sure. It's not set up that way. People can just show up if they're interested."

"Well, hopefully they'll have someone knowledgeable leading it. I could show you two around if you'd rather."

Fiona felt a moment of panic. She could already see she would be the third wheel. "I really don't want to put you to that trouble. Thanks, but it's fine."

Well, it's up to you."

Was she imagining it or did Béatrice look relieved?

On the walk to the museum, the sidewalk wasn't wide enough for three, so Béatrice took Emily's arm, making comments over her shoulder to Fiona and occasionally making side comments in French to Emily. By the time they'd arrived, Fiona was more than ready for Béatrice to be on her way.

"Looks like that woman over there is holding a sign for my tour company. Emily, do you want to join me?"

"Sure. I'll be there in a moment."

Fiona left the two standing together, their heads almost touching, and hurried over to the group. The young tour guide looked annoyed at Fiona's late arrival and continued her introduction to the museum. Emily appeared a moment later, and she and Fiona trailed along at the back of the group as they started off.

"Béatrice told me the couple who founded the museum were also the founders of the first department store in Paris called La Samaritaine."

"When was that?" Fiona grudgingly asked. She didn't want to be interested in anything Béatrice had to say.

"1869. It was a brilliant idea. The department store offered, for the first time, a way for someone to buy new clothes and other products at affordable prices."

"Isn't that when you said the middle class was just forming?"

"Yes, exactly. Their target audience. No wonder they were so successful. And it's a fun tie to our discussion the other night. So I'd say it's perfect timing to visit this museum for the first time." Emily's eyes were warm, and Fiona flushed.

Forty-five minutes later, they were back at the entrance. "Do you have plans now? I'm starving as usual, and I know a good place near here."

Fiona laughed. "Seems you know a good place near just about everywhere. Sure, lead the way." She was relieved Béatrice had not been mentioned again.

They chose an outside table, sitting next to each other and looking out at the street, and ordered salads and glasses of wine. "My feet and my head were both ready for a break." Fiona said as she thumped down.

Emily laughed. "How is your head? Feeling better?"

"Much. The paracetamol and the walking did their magic."

Emily reached over to brush a leaf out of Fiona's hair. Her hand lingered, and she suddenly leaned forward to brush Fiona's lips in a light kiss.

Astonished, Fiona's first thought was to pull away, but Emily immediately leaned back, and continued her discussion about the museum as if nothing had happened. Fiona looked around nervously to see if anyone was watching them and noticed that many of the tables were occupied by either two men or two women, and some were obviously couples. No one showed the slightest interest in Emily and Fiona, and Fiona reached up to briefly touch her lip where it still tingled.

The waiter brought their food, and they talked about life in their respective cities. They both laughed as they admitted neither had ever visited the other's hometown.

"So, what are your plans for the rest of the day?" Emily asked, as the waiter set down their espressos.

"My friend Jane and I are going to a champagne tasting at around six, then getting dinner somewhere nearby. Fancy joining us?"

"Unfortunately, I can't."

Fiona's stomach clenched. She tried to sound casual. "Oh, plans with Béatrice?"

Emily looked surprised. "No, one of the priests at Notre Dame has agreed to show me some documents from the archives this afternoon, and I have no idea how long I'll be. With the fire and all of the upheaval right now, I'm lucky to have been able to get some time with him, and I'll want to stay as long as he lets me." She paused. "I'd really like to see you again before you head home. What about tomorrow afternoon? Tomorrow is your last day, right?"

"My last full day. I leave Saturday morning, so yes, let's plan on that. But I don't want to interfere with your research time, so be honest if that's an issue."

"It's no problem. I'll be finished by early afternoon." With a wry smile, Emily added, "Do you suppose you could give me your phone number this time?"

Fiona blushed. "Of course."

"I'm just teasing you. I like seeing you blush." Emily reached over and kissed Fiona again, and this time, her lips lingered. Her breath was warm, and smelled like coffee, and Fiona, at first startled, let herself relax into the kiss. They eventually drew apart, and Emily's smile made her stomach do flip flops.

When they stood, Emily gave Fiona a hug, embracing her for a long moment before releasing her. Fiona noticed that Emily's head came to just above her shoulder.

"Thank you for coming to find me. I've had a great time today," Fiona said nervously, fiddling with her backpack for a moment.

"Me, too. Okay, I've got to get going or I'll be late. I'll text you later?" Emily set off, stopping briefly at the corner for a final smile and wave.

Fiona started to walk back toward her hotel, reaching up to again touch her lips. She felt like her whole world had turned upside down and seeing Emily in the hotel lobby felt like a lifetime ago. She needed time to work through it all. A brisk walk through the Marais for some window shopping and then back to the hotel would be just the ticket.

Chapter 12

By the time Jane finished her breakfast, she was feeling herself again. She spent an hour at the apartment carefully filling out the school applications, then set off for the Left Bank, enjoying the meander through winding streets. Letting herself drift from store to store, she found a set of cheese knives with brightly colored handles of orange, green, red and yellow for Kallie, scarves for friends, and earrings for her two sisters.

Starting to feel hungry, she squeezed into the last open seat in a crowded café off the Boulevard Saint Germain. After ordering, she surreptitiously looked around at the other customers, noticing suddenly she was twisting her wedding ring. She considered for a long moment, then took it off and put it in her purse.

Ten minutes later, her glass of red wine and her open-faced sandwich arrived, a *croque madame*. It was piping hot, with the cheese nicely browned over a thick slice of ham, and a sunny side up egg a bright splash of orange on top. Next to it was a mound of green salad, dressed with the ubiquitous café vinaigrette.

Jane closed her eyes as she took her first bite. The egg yolk blended with the slightly salty Gruyère cheese, which in turn blended with the creaminess of the béchamel sauce. The crusty bread beneath offered contrast to all the creaminess, followed by the tart bite of the vinaigrette and crunch of the lettuce. The simplest of dishes, yet multi-layered in flavor and texture.

As she ate, Jane invented stories about the various groups seated nearby. Next to her was a table with four businessmen, all nearly identical in dark suits and crisp, white shirts. In her imagination, they all worked for a financial services firm or a bank, taking a break for a quick lunch. Beyond them were a couple and their son, obviously tourists, dressed in brightly colored clothes and sneakers. From the mother's blond hair, and their tans, Jane concluded they were American, and from the west coast.

Her favorite was an older French couple, the man elegant in a brown jacket and tie, the woman in a cream-colored blouse and patterned scarf. The waiter had greeted them warmly and motioned them to a table in the corner, whisking away the *Reserved* sign as he moved the table out so that they could sit side by side on the bench and look out.

Jane could hear snippets of the couple's conversation, and she loved their quiet, comfortable banter. For a moment, she felt a pang of loneliness. She would have loved to have someone sitting with her, discussing whatever exhibit they'd visited that day or concert they'd attended. She and Jack had spent many evenings together at events of all sorts and always enjoyed discussing afterward what they'd liked and disliked. But that was in Boston. It was time to acknowledge that if the venue were Paris, or some other foreign city, that person would never be Jack.

She wondered what he was doing right now. It was

early morning in Boston, so he'd be heading into the office soon. Maybe talk to the other partners about taking off early for a golf game tomorrow. The golf club was an important part of his business networking agenda, both on the course and off. There were always members to meet and greet and Friday evenings he often stayed for dinner at the grill, so he and his partners could enjoy their customary burgers and beers and come up with strategies for the latest client's portfolio of office buildings.

God, that all sounded so boring. But that was Jack's life and he loved it. And she'd enjoyed it too. They had some very good friends, and Boston had always been a wonderful place for theater and the arts. She'd always had plenty to do, with her own job, with raising Kallie, and with the many charity functions she and Jack attended. But she realized now that the last couple of years she'd been yearning for more. Looking forward to expanding their horizons once Kallie was settled and Jack could hand more responsibilities of the daily work routine off to his team. Looking back now, she should have known things would not change. Routine for Jack meant stability and security. Routine for her, at least in her early life, had been a rare commodity as an Air Force brat who moved every three years. So, Boston, in those early married years, had felt solid and predictable in a good way. It was only recently as she began to look forward to exploring other places again that it had started to feel confining rather than reassuring. Something to tolerate rather than something to revel in. Jack's pronouncement had been a shock, but behind her anger and her fear—if she were being honest with herself—was there also relief?

She looked around at the murmuring couples, the laughter, the busy city street so different from her suburban view. And she loved it. *Even the cigarette smoke,* she thought ruefully. She was not sorry to have ended up here. She would apply to the cooking schools, and in the meantime, she wouldn't let herself brood.

She would, instead, embrace this new life and what better way to start than to indulge with dessert? She chose a lemon tart and with her first bite, she was transported. What was that extra flavor? She closed her eyes and held a bite of the tart filling in her mouth, but the flavor eluded her. What *was* it? She motioned to the waiter, and giving him her brightest smile, told him the tart was delicious, but that she couldn't quite place the flavors in the filling. Did he by any chance know what was in it?

He assured her it was made in-house and that he would go ask the chef. She went back to watching the passersby and trying to overhear the various conversations around her. Someone behind her cleared his throat and she turned to see what the waiter had found out, but instead of the waiter, it was Bernard, in his white chef's coat.

"You?" His dark eyes were sparkling.

"You?" she responded, nearly choking on the last of her wine. "So, this is where you work."

"*Oui.*" His eyes lingered on her smiling lips. "I was told that a customer had a question about the lemon tart?"

"Yes, there's a flavor here I can't quite place."

He raised one eyebrow. "And you wish for me to share my secret recipe?"

Jane felt flustered by his direct gaze, and the feelings it was generating in the pit of her stomach.

When she didn't answer right away, he laughed. "I'm teasing you but take a guess."

"Okay. It's an herb, I think. Wait a minute. Thyme, maybe?"

"Yes, exactly right."

"It just came to me." She smiled up at him, and she noticed a small spot on the lower right side of his chin he'd missed while shaving.

"You have a good sense of taste."

"It's a silly game I like to play. To challenge myself to figure out the flavors when I try something new."

"By the way, I'm sorry I had to run off the other day. One of the other chefs called in sick and I had to come in to take his shift."

"I totally understand. It's lucky you were so close."

Bernard looked back where someone was motioning to him from the bar area. "I'm sorry, but I have to go. I always seem to be running away." His eyes looked regretful. *"Au revoir."*

"Au revoir."

She lingered over her espresso, hoping he might come out of the kitchen again. She couldn't believe she'd now run into him twice. Watching his face when she'd taken a bite of the tart, she'd seen his pleasure at her enjoyment of it and it had sent her imagination spinning.

She smiled to herself, then signaled to the waiter for the bill, slipping the restaurant card in her purse. She might have to find an excuse to come back. Her phone buzzed to remind her about the wine tasting and she pulled it out to send Fiona a text.

What did u decide? Interested in the champagne tasting?

Definitely. Meet at your apt? Can u send the address?

Perfect. Should be there in 30 mins or so.

Fiona was waiting at the front door as Jane rounded the corner. "Hope I didn't keep you waiting," Jane said breathlessly.

"No, I just got here myself."

"How was the Marais tour?" Jane asked as they

climbed the two flights.

"Interesting. I just went to the first part which was the Cognacq-Jay Museum. Have you been?"

"No, never."

"One of the couples from the cooking class was also there. I hadn't realized they'd bought the same package as I did. It was a good group." Fiona opened her mouth again, then shut it as if she'd changed her mind about what she was going to say.

"That's fun Who was it?"

"The younger British couple in the back of our class. How about you? Did you have a good day?"

"I did, but let's walk and talk or we'll be late. Véronique also said she'll join us for dinner. She suggested a crepe place nearby."

Just then, Jane's phone buzzed and reading the message she stopped short and did a fist pump into the air.

"What's happened?"

"It's a text from Véronique. She says there's an email to me from her chef friend at one of the schools. I can't believe it!"

Chapter 13

It was mid-afternoon and Véronique stood for a moment at the mirror in the ladies' room, checking for anything caught in her teeth before setting off for the large conference room. The President, Jean Gauthier, was planning to attend her weekly London meeting for an update, and she fervently hoped everyone on her team would come fully prepared. Anyone looking less than professional would reflect badly on her as their manager. Some senior staff would also be giving their reports and she prayed that all was proceeding as planned.

She nervously entered the room, nodding to Claude Bernier, the head of Construction and Logistics. They'd already dealt with several crises, and she'd appreciated his no-nonsense approach. David, sitting next to him, winked at her as she entered, and beyond him sat Camille, whose bright red nails were tapping impatiently on the table, her expression unreadable. Véronique hoped she wouldn't make trouble. The last person on that side was Francois Mercier, who had been working directly with Jeanne on her team on the baked goods orders. Sitting on the opposite side of the table were her various direct reports.

Véronique moved to the head of the table and cleared her throat. "Good afternoon, everyone. With just two weeks until the opening, we all have a lot on our plates, so please keep your updates short. Any problems requiring a longer conversation will be set aside and discussed at the end. Any questions? Great, Claude, can you start us off with a construction update?"

"*Bonjour tout le monde,*" Claude said, standing. "As you know, the building we are going to occupy was a grocery store before, so we have some basic infrastructure in place already which has helped immensely. You will see in front of you the final layout of the various departments within the store itself. Please send me a note afterward if you have questions or issues on the placement decisions. The general shelving is now in place for all departments, and we have begun the work on the areas requiring special refrigerated shelving. The window display areas are finished as well, and we've built in easy access panels since Véronique will be rotating different displays through them each month. Everything is on schedule."

"*Merci, Claude.* Jeanne?"

Jeanne spent a couple of minutes shuffling her papers, and Véronique could see she was nervous with such senior members of staff in attendance. She finally smiled tremulously, and in a quiet voice, said, "We've scheduled the first packaged food deliveries to arrive this weekend, and all of the fresh produce, meats, and cheeses have been ordered but will be scheduled to arrive just before we open. The bread and other baked goods will also arrive just before we open." This with a nod to Francois.

"Thank you, Jeanne. Marc, do we have all the permits and licenses in place?"

"Yes. We were waiting on our EORI number — which is required to import goods into the UK — " this last addition said with a look at Jean Gauthier, "but it came in last night when they'd confirmed they'd received the final paperwork."

Camille interrupted, her throaty voice overriding his softer tone. "Excuse me, Véronique, how about the process for paying the duty and VAT taxes? Is that taken care of?"

"Yes, Camille." *Though I'm not sure what business it is of yours.* Véronique kept her voice calm and assured, though she was seething. "All import declarations need a commodity code which we received yesterday. We also hired a customs agent to make sure we don't miss anything. Anything else, Marc?" Marc shook his head, looking relieved to be taken out of the spotlight.

Véronique turned back to Camille. "Camille, could we have your update on public relations and media?" Her sharp tone was not lost on Camille, who ignored it, taking an extra moment to smile at Monsieur Gauthier. Véronique couldn't help feeling gleeful when she noticed a smudge of lipstick on Camille's front tooth.

"All is well in hand. We have confirmations from a local news network as well as several independent food critics that they will be at the opening." Jean Gauthier seemed to be paying rapt attention and Véronique wondered cynically if it was to her words or her cleavage.

David then gave his update on the website and the ongoing email campaign, with a couple of sample slides, and then Véronique opened it to questions.

"That went well," David murmured, falling into step with Véronique as they filed out.

"Yes, but you heard Camille trying to sabotage me. What is she doing asking about VAT taxes, for God's sake?"

"Don't let her get to you. You've got things well in

hand and everyone knows it."

"She needs to mind her own business."

"Okay, okay, just ignore her."

Once Véronique was back in her office, she sank into her seat and sent Jane and Fiona a quick text.

Thank God I'm seeing you two tonight. What a day.

Three hours later, she stood, flexing her shoulders which were tight after so much time hunched over the computer. It was time to go meet Jane and Fiona and eat some delicious crepes.

*****

Once they had ordered, Jane turned to Véronique. "Véronique, what was that text about? Obviously, something not going as well as you'd hoped."

Véronique sighed. "We had our weekly update meeting and Camille, Queen Bitch in Charge of Media, kept trying to sabotage me."

"Wow. Who is this woman?"

"She, David and I all started at the same time, and I swear she's had it in for me since the first day."

"What did she do this time?"

"Well, several of the top management people were in the meeting today, including the President, so there was extra pressure on everyone, and she asks, out of the blue, something about taxes which has nothing to do with her or with media." She laughed wryly. "I'm certainly not saying I don't make mistakes. In fact, I *had* forgotten some paperwork the other day which was why I had to leave the café after our class, but *she* doesn't need to know that." She sighed. "There *is* a lot to keep track of, and that's a part of this job I don't care about at all."

"Really?" Fiona asked, her eyes gleaming. "I actually like that part of my job. Because I oversee the sales group, it's up to me to figure out the sequencing and timetables for the deliveries and installations of all the window blinds orders. Each time is different, and I like to challenge myself to keep making it more efficient. It's almost like a giant Sudoku puzzle where every number has to be in its correct spot. For me, every order has to end up exactly where and when it's supposed to."

"You like that stuff, Fiona? That is what stresses me out the most."

"What's your favorite part, then?"

"Lots of other things. Walking the site with Claude Bernier, our construction guy, and seeing it all come together. I love interviewing the prospective customers to decide what to order." For a moment, Véronique looked embarrassed. "And probably my favorite part is anything having to do with design decisions. I've loved working on the front window displays for instance. That probably sounds silly to you."

"Not at all, and see? That's something I would be terrible at." Fiona had become quite animated. "The creative side scares me to death. Give me numbers, and times, and delivery sequences. Give me logical variables that I can put together and I'm happy as a clam."

"Jane what do you think? You don't think that stuff is fun, do you?"

"Sorry, but actually I do. My first job was working with a team who put real estate deals together, and I loved that. Like Fiona was saying about her orders, each deal had different elements, different processes, and different final results, but each time, the various pieces had to all get done when and where they were supposed to."

Fiona grinned. "But wait. We haven't even talked about the things each time that aren't in my control that can still bollox it all up. Like a traffic jam or bad weather."

"Yeah, absolutely. For our deals, it might be a zoning question, or the financing suddenly goes sideways, or there's an unexpected issue with a neighboring property. But we'd work around that stuff and when everything fell into place, what a great feeling of accomplishment." Jane and Fiona smiled broadly at each other.

Véronique shook her head in disbelief. "You are both crazy."

Jane laughed. "Sorry, Véronique. We're ganging up against you this time. Sounds like the most important thing to learn out of this is that next time you'll want to be sure you have someone on your team to delegate that stuff to, then you can focus on the design elements you love."

Véronique grinned. "Either of you want to volunteer? Oh, wait, Jane will be a chef by then. Speaking of that, what did my friend Michel send you about the school?"

"I completely forgot to check." They both looked at her in disbelief and she laughed. "Okay, that's a lie. I've read it about a dozen times and was just waiting for you to ask. Here, let me find it and read it to you."

Jane opened her phone and when she looked up, her eyes were bright with excitement. "I quote- 'I have received your application as well as a note from Véronique Moreau about your qualifications and would like to inform you that we have had a cancellation in the course that's starting next Monday. You have been provisionally accepted, subject to successfully completing a written and a practical test next Thursday.' What does that mean? What do I need to know? What kind of practical test? What if my French isn't good enough?"

"Slow down, Jane." Véronique held up her hand laughing. "I'll send you the names of the reference books I mentioned to help with vocabulary for the written test. The practical test will probably be something simple, like making an omelet. You can handle it, I'm sure."

"I can't believe this is really happening. It has been a crazy whirlwind of a week. Oh, wait! I haven't even told you about two other things that happened. Véronique, what other top management were in your meeting this afternoon?"

Véronique looked at her, confused, but said, "Claude Bernier that I mentioned earlier, David, as the technical expert, and Francois Mercier, who oversees all of our baked goods. Why?"

Now Jane was practically jumping up and down in her seat. "This is such a crazy coincidence; you're not going to believe it. So, as I told Fiona, I have been going to visit some of my old college day haunts and yesterday I decided to go see if the bakery that belonged to my French boyfriend's family was still there. The first cool thing is that it still exists, though his family doesn't own it anymore, but even cooler is that as I was eating my croissant at the park, my old boyfriend showed up!"

"That is amazing!" Fiona said loudly and a couple of heads turned toward them. She lowered her voice. "Sorry, that's smashing. Really."

"It is but wait until you hear who it is." Jane paused dramatically, then said, "Francois Mercier."

Véronique's mouth fell open. "What? The same Francois Mercier who heads our baked goods division?"

"Yes! Francois went to business school because he liked the numbers more than the actual baking. Can you believe that? He spoke very warmly of you, by the way, Véronique."

"I can't believe it!" Véronique was shaking her head.

"And that's not all. The *other* thing that happened is that I ran into Chef Bernard, not once but twice!"

"Okay, this calls for another glass of wine," Véronique said and motioned to the waiter.

"I know—I couldn't believe it either." Jane described seeing him at the store, and then again at the café. "Isn't that crazy?"

"Did you tell him you liked his *coq au vin* and that you want a private lesson on how to cook it?" Véronique teased.

Jane blushed. "No, I didn't. But I did find out he's from Dijon and that he makes a delicious lemon tart."

"It sounds like you might have another reason to stick around Paris for a while," Véronique said.

"I can't even kid about that. I've still got a lot to figure out with Jack."

"You're right. Sorry. Completely selfishly, I hope you stay in Paris so I can ask your advice on work issues and eventually on how to raise kids."

"I will admit to you two I also really hope it works out." Jane felt guilty saying it out loud, but it was definitely what her heart was already telling her.

Chapter 14

The dinner with Véronique and Jane, like the time spent with Emily, had reminded Fiona how nice it was to have people to talk to about things that really mattered to you and how isolated she'd become. The discussion about Véronique's store opening had been particularly interesting. Describing out loud the things she liked about her job at the factory had brought into focus the sort of work she might look for if she did decide to move on. It had made her realize that even though she felt nervous about having been in the same place her entire career, the skills she'd learned there were transferable.

From Véronique's description, the logistics at Bon Gout were just a different sort of puzzle, but the skillset required was the same. If they were successful at this first London store, there would certainly be more openings, in London and possibly even in other cities. Why couldn't she be a part of something like that? It was an exciting prospect. Much more challenging and interesting than her current job.

And the person she wanted to talk through it all with was Emily. She quickened her pace toward the Luxembourg

Gardens where they'd arranged to meet. Emily would be dispassionate and offer logical pros and cons, but she would also understand the guilt weighing Fiona down.

Emily, who already seemed to understand her better than many people she'd known much longer. Emily, who she already felt so at ease with. Emily, whose unexpected appearance at the hotel had touched Fiona deeply. She didn't remember the last time someone had been that interested in spending time with her. Someone who also seemed to share so many of her interests and values.

And then Emily had kissed her, and she had been startled, but after what she'd surmised earlier watching her with Beatrice, not entirely unexpected. When she thought back, there'd been something there from the start — a tension — an attraction. But it was something that Fiona had not let herself see. It had awakened something in her she'd buried when she was eighteen. Now, she let her thoughts turn back to that time.

She'd always been bored with school, tolerating it rather than enjoying it, and had only survived because of her two best mates, Louise and Jennifer. The three girls had been thick as thieves, doing everything together.

That particular year, Fiona had been asked to attend the school dance by Gerald Harwood, a boy in her economics course with large black spectacles and bad acne. Louise was going with the star of the rugby team, and Jennifer with her long-time boyfriend.

The dance had been held at the school cafeteria and the six of them showed up at the dance slightly tipsy, due to the cheap wine Gerald had smuggled into the large black taxi.

Fiona had excused herself to go to the loo after the third dance, and she and Louise and Jennifer had giggled and talked about how the evening was going. Louise said she wanted a quick smoke, so after leaving the bathroom, Jennifer returned to the dance, and Louise and Fiona made their way through the crowd to a side door. They stood for a moment in the cool evening air, enjoying the solitude after the noise and activity inside.

Louise smoked in silence, then crushed her cigarette under her shoe before turning to Fiona. "So how is it *really* going?"

"Honestly, not bad. At least he's almost my height so I don't feel like the Jolly Green Giant," Fiona laughed.

"That *does* make it nicer for sure. Why are these boys so short? Look—you and I are almost the same height." With that, Louise stepped up so that their faces were almost touching, holding her hand above their heads to measure the difference in height.

Her breath smelled slightly of cigarette smoke and wine. Her eyes looked large and dark, and Fiona suddenly noticed the tiny freckles on the bridge of her nose. She gazed into her friend's eyes and saw a change there that she was sure was reflected in her own. Louise's hand dropped from its position of measuring their heights to softly caress Fiona's cheek.

"You look lovely tonight, by the way," Louise had said, barely above a whisper.

Fiona froze, her heart thumping. She felt the urge to lean forward and kiss Louise, but she jerked back, shaking. What was she thinking? Louise was her best mate—had been since they were thirteen. Why was she feeling like this? Could she blame it on the wine?

Louise had looked at her for another moment, then dropped her hand to her side, and Fiona had turned away, embarrassed.

They had walked back in silence and rejoined the

others. Fiona had told Gerald she didn't feel well and asked him to take her home. She and Louise had never spoken about that moment afterward and after graduation, Louise left Liverpool for a job in Birmingham.

Fiona had never told anyone about what had happened. Her mother was staunch Catholic, herding the family off to Mass every Sunday, then attending Mass daily in her later years. Her rigid standards of morality would never have tolerated such a conversation.

Her mother was always regaling her with stories of the wild behavior of women during the war years and talking about how morals had completely disappeared during the 60's, with everyone on drugs and engaging in 'free love'. To her mother, sex was a necessary evil, not something any normal, decent person would find enjoyable, so Fiona was not surprised when, the few times she'd had sex, she'd been left feeling disappointed and unfulfilled.

She'd never really had any long-term relationships and on the few dates she'd gone on, she was always either tongue-tied, searching desperately for a topic of mutual interest, or bored because her date would drone on and on about football, or about how much they hated their jobs.

She'd never bothered much with makeup or worrying about her hair, which she kept short because it then required very little maintenance. Friends over the years had admonished her to do herself up more, but Fiona didn't see the point. She was who she was, and other people's opinion on her appearance didn't matter to her in the least. She'd always been well-liked at work, was considered to be a good storyteller, and was always ready to laugh, including at herself.

She'd always attributed her lack of success with men to a lack of social graces, but now, for the first time, she let herself consider a completely different conclusion.

She was no longer a naïve girl of eighteen. She felt at ease with Emily in a way she'd never experienced before. She didn't know what their relationship would become, but she did know she wanted to spend more time figuring it out. Living in different cities would make things more complicated. But after this week of trying—and succeeding— in doing things she'd never tried before, she wasn't afraid of the challenge.

Fiona turned the corner and smiled broadly when she saw Emily standing by the gate. Emily came towards her, waving and pointing further up the street. "Let's grab a coffee or tea from Starbucks, and don't give me that look. I'm suggesting it because they do takeaway, and we can then go sit in the park."

Fiona laughed. "A perfect Parisian adaptation of an American concept."

Cups in hand, they made their way through the gates and to the large pond in the center of the park. They chose two of the metal chairs near the pond that had been warmed by the afternoon sun and sat, drinking slowly and watching the children race back and forth, wooden sailboats clutched in their hands. Their cries and laughter filled the air with unadulterated joy.

Fiona felt the tension leave her shoulders and she turned to face the sun, shutting her eyes to simply enjoy its warmth. Emily reached over to take Fiona's hand, and Fiona squeezed it, reveling in the comfort it gave her.

"Have you ever thought about having children?" Emily asked. Startled, Fiona opened her eyes to see Emily gazing out at the children by the pond.

"Um. Not really," Fiona said. "My parents weren't exactly a great role model. You?"

"I would have liked to. There was a moment when I thought it might be possible..." Emily's voice faded away, and the sounds of the children's laughter washed over them.

"You mean when you were with Béatrice?" Fiona asked tentatively.

"No, not Béatrice. That was just a short fling at a moment when I was desperately unhappy in my life. It would never have been a long-term thing. No, this was years ago, just after I finished my degree. I was in Oxford on a research fellowship that summer and that's where I met Gwen. It was at a function held by the Women's Auxiliary. We talked so long I missed an important meeting." Emily laughed quietly. "I gave her a hard time about that for years." She fell silent again, seemingly lost in her memories, but then shook her head slightly, and continued. "We had twenty wonderful years. At various times, we talked about children—either having one ourselves or adopting—but the time never seemed quite right, and then, when we'd finally decided to adopt, we found out she had a brain tumor. I lost her six weeks later. That was two years ago."

Fiona sat, stunned.

Emily was still holding her hand. "Gwen's death was hard, and I vowed I wouldn't let myself be hurt like that again. I've been lonely, and sad, but except for that brief time with Béatrice haven't done anything about it. Then I saw you sitting at the café, reading one of my favorite books, and I told myself it was a sign—the Universe telling me it was time to start living again."

The sounds of the children gradually died down as families gathered their belongings and headed home.

"I am so sorry you had to go through that."

"I didn't mean to get so maudlin, but I wanted you to know." Emily smiled and they sat quietly as the shadows gathered around them.

Chapter 15

Fiona cast one final glance around the room. Her suitcase sat at the end of the bed, ready for the morning. She reached for her nicest pair of trousers and pulled them on, adding a cream-colored blouse and the scarf she'd bought the day of the cooking class.

She stood for a moment in front of the mirror to look at herself critically. The water in Paris was doing wonders for her hair. Not a single frizz. For the first time, she wished for a bit of mascara to make her eyes look larger. A couple of times during the afternoon she'd caught Emily looking at her with an expression that both thrilled and terrified her.

Fiona pulled her new leather coat from the closet. It was too warm to wear during the day, but she thought she could pull it off with the cooler evening air. Slipping her arms into the sleeves, she turned once more to the mirror, and was pleased to see reflected a confident woman heading out for a delicious dinner in Paris. She picked up her purse and the gift she'd found for Emily, then made her way downstairs and out to the street, buoyed by the newly appreciative glance from the clerk at the reception desk.

Thirty minutes later, she was walking the last block to the restaurant. It looked friendly and inviting, with tables covered in bright green and white checked tablecloths.

The windows across the front were folded back, and a soft breeze brought the noise of an occasional motorcycle, or honking horn, but the restaurant's location on a small side street meant that the general city hubbub was reduced to a low background hum.

Emily was already seated at one of the inside tables and rose to give Fiona a kiss on each cheek. Her lips lingered for an extra moment, and Fiona felt warmed by the subtle message it sent. "I love your jacket. You don't even look British," she said with a mischievous smile.

Fiona felt herself flush with pleasure. "Well, there's a story behind that."

"Can't wait to hear it." Emily swept her arm around the restaurant. "Do you like what you see?"

Fiona looked directly at Emily for a moment, then, feeling quite bold, replied, "Very much."

Emily looked surprised for a moment before laughing out loud. Fiona took off her coat and they both sat, Emily still chuckling.

"The restaurant is owned by Thomas, the chef, and his wife, Marie who you just met. I love them and this restaurant because they're not stuck on lots of pomp and circumstance. They just want to serve delicious food."

"I can't wait." Fiona looked around for Marie, then back at Emily. "Is she going to bring menus? Or is there a sandwich board listing the specials of the day?"

Emily shook her head with a small smile. "Do you have any allergies?"

"No." Now Fiona was confused.

"Good, because there are no menus. You have a choice

of either two courses, which has a starter and a main dish, or three, which includes dessert. They won't tell us what we're eating beforehand. They'd rather we taste it, try to guess what it is, and then tell them what we think of it."

"I've never eaten at a restaurant like this," Fiona said, grinning, "but I'm very excited to give it a go."

"Would you like the two-course, or the three-course with dessert?"

"With dessert, please. I'm starving."

"Me, too."

Marie took their order, and Emily asked her to bring a bottle of whatever wine would go best with their meal. It was like no experience Fiona had ever had at home. She loved the feeling the chef was preparing something special just for her.

When the wine arrived, they toasted their new friendship, and Fiona reached down for the gift bag.

"What's this?"

"Something I found wandering around the Marais."

Emily reached in and carefully pulled out the tissue-wrapped rectangle. "It's heavy," she said, smiling in anticipation.

"I hope you like it."

It was a large book and Emily opened it gently, the heavily embossed, leather cover stiff with age. Inside were delicate, hand-drawn illustrations showing different views of Notre Dame. Each was covered by a fine sheet of tissue paper. Emily carefully turned back each layer as she turned the pages. "Ohhhhh..." she sighed, reverently stopping several times to examine individual pictures. She looked up at Fiona and her eyes shone. "This is beautiful. Where in the world you find it?"

"In the Saint Paul area of the Mar~' very dusty antique shop," Fiona said, d reaction.

Emily reached for Fiona's hand. "Thank you *so* much. I can't even begin to express how much this means."

Marie suddenly appeared at Emily's side, bringing the first course on a black plate. It was a small piece of white fish, its crispy skin forming a decorative crescent over thin curled slices of a yellow vegetable accompanied by a small, pickled corn cob.

"This looks delicious," Emily said. "Any ideas of what kind of fish it might be?"

"Not a clue. I'm only an expert on one kind—fish and chips from the pub." Fiona tentatively cut off one bite and raised it to her lips. "This is good. Very mild." She then tried the vegetables. "This is good, too. I never eat enough vegetables at home."

As the meal progressed, she was impressed by how good Emily was at figuring out what things were, and also at how much she liked most of the things she tried. It was another way this trip had changed her, she realized with a start, and wondered if she would be happy going back to her regular diet of pub food.

Fiona couldn't wait to see what came out for dessert, and with a flourish, the waiter set it in front of them. A bright green sorbet, made from green tea, sat atop fresh strawberries and sprinkled chocolate pieces, surrounded by small florets of whipped cream. Fiona didn't love the green tea sorbet but was proud of herself for not grimacing when she tried it, and the fresh strawberries and chocolate more than made up for it.

The evening flew by. Emily told Fiona stories about her childhood in the small town of Padstow in Cornwall, and that she would be heading down there later in the summer to stay in the tiny cottage her parents had left her.

Fiona told Emily more about her job at the factory and

about Kevin pressuring her to take on more responsibility. She talked about the conversation with Jane and Véronique and how it had opened her eyes to other possibilities.

"Fiona, I think you should follow your heart on this. I understand your loyalty to your family, but you need to have as your first priority what *you* want."

"I know you're right, but it's going to take me some time to figure out how to do that. I *am* getting there," she added at Emily's sceptic look. "I promise. And who knows? I might even ask Véronique about Bon Gout if the London opening goes well. What about you? How have your meetings been going at Notre Dame?"

"Very well, actually." Emily's eyes were bright. "The priests have been incredibly helpful, and we've found several documents they've let me copy to take back to Oxford." She reached over to stroke Fiona's cheek, and Fiona leaned into her touch briefly. "But let's not talk about work anymore. This is our last night in this magical city."

"This meal was incredible," Fiona effused as they got their coats and made their way to the door. "You were absolutely right. And I loved the whole format of having the chef decide what to make. I will never forget this evening."

"It's not over yet," Emily said as she took Fiona's arm. "It's too beautiful a night to simply go home." Her tone turned accusing. "Be honest. Have you been out this late any night this week?"

Sheepishly, Fiona admitted she hadn't, and arm in arm, they strolled down several quiet streets until they reached the Seine. Ahead of them stretched a softly lit bridge, the light from its yellow lanterns glinting off the water flowing below. Emily led Fiona out to the middle of the bridge, and they gazed out over the water, their arms touching.

Turning to comment on the view, Fiona f

face inches from hers, and suddenly, Emily leaned in to kiss her. At first surprised, Fiona found herself kissing her back. Emily's breath tasted faintly of chocolate, and her lips felt soft against Fiona's. For a moment, she thought of Gerald's farewell kiss that long ago evening, and how she'd wanted it to end as quickly as possible. She'd never imagined kissing someone could feel like this—simultaneously take her breath away and overwhelming her. After a long moment she pulled away, but then found herself grinning foolishly. She closed her eyes to lock the memory into her brain for later.

They started walking again, and moved towards the sound of laughter that was tumbling out of a nearby café. A young couple vacated their outside table just as Fiona and Emily arrived, and Emily pounced on it. She ordered them each a Grand Marnier. The alcohol warmed Fiona's throat as she swallowed. She'd never tasted it before, and she loved its sharp, tangy hint of ripe orange.

In contrast to the quiet street they'd left behind, they were now surrounded by noise and activity: people on the bridge; couples and families strolling along the street in front of the café; and of course, in the café itself. The energy was palpable, and Fiona realized how much she'd missed this sort of social interaction. In recent years, the few times she did allow herself an evening out, she would always beg off early, feeling guilty for letting herself simply relax for a little while. A quick glance at her phone told her it was almost midnight.

"Is it always like this on a Friday night?"

"Always," Emily said, her hand lightly covering Fiona's. "Parisians love to be out socializing."

Fiona couldn't stop smiling. It was hard to believe she was actually in Paris, enjoying a nightcap with a new friend with whom she'd shared a gourmet meal. A week ago, this would have been unimaginable.

Emily glanced at her phone, and with a voice full of regret, she announced, "We do have a train to catch in the morning, so we should probably call it a night." She motioned for the bill, then reached over to tuck a lock of Fiona's hair behind her ear. "I've loved showing you around one of my favorite cities. I hope we can meet back here soon. There's so much more we need to see and do."

"I can't wait," Fiona stammered, feeling it sounded inadequate, but not able to manage more.

At the metro, Emily leaned in close to kiss Fiona on both cheeks, lingering again for a long moment. "See you tomorrow. Half past nine at Gare du Nord. Sleep well."

Fiona floated down to the metro platform and then on to her hotel, her mind filled with the sights and sensations of the evening. She barely remembered to set her alarm before falling into a blissful sleep.

Chapter 16

"What a flight," Angela said as she plopped down in the seat next to Jane. "I had this man next to me snoring incredibly loudly, and a woman behind me who talked to her friend the whole time." Angela stopped talking only long enough to take a breath before adding, "You look fabulous, by the way."

Jane shook her head, smiling. She hadn't let herself really believe it when Angela had announced she was coming to check on her. It had turned out to be perfect timing, with Angela arriving the day after Fiona had left to return to Liverpool. Now, here she was, sitting in Sylvie's café, her signature Dolce & Gabbana raincoat folded over the back of the chair.

"You look pretty amazing yourself. You do not look like you've been on a plane for seven hours."

"Believe me, with all the craziness around me, it felt like longer. I'm glad it doesn't show." Angela, as usual, managed to fill her own space and more besides. Though only five foot three in her stockinged feet, she became the center of attention in whatever room she entered, her bright blue eyes missing nothing of whatever was happening around her.

Sylvie came over to be introduced and to get Angela's order, then Angela turned back to Jane. "Tell me absolutely everything. How are you doing? Don't you just love the apartment? Tell me more about Fiona and Véronique, and the cooking class. What did you cook?"

The questions came fast and furious.

"Whoa. One thing at a time." Jane laughed at Angela's exuberance. God how she'd missed her. She waited until Angela had stopped exclaiming over how incredible the croissant was, and the coffee, and the cute men, then answered her questions one by one.

"And have you heard from Jack?"

"No, and I didn't really expect to."

"I've been spying on him a little on Facebook and he and Barbara definitely look like an item."

Jane felt a jolt of anger followed quickly by regret. Regret for not trying harder, but also regret for *him* not trying harder.

"I texted Kallie and went up to see her in her new apartment." Angela's voice broke through her thoughts and she started.

"Don't worry," Angela added at Jane's panicked look, "I'm keeping with our story that you and I are spending some girl time here in Paris."

"So, I assume Jack hasn't said anything to her either?"

"I assume not. What's he going to say? That he refused to come to Paris? That he'd rather hang out with some bimbo from work?"

"Angela, don't be too harsh with him."

"Why not? He devastated my best friend!"

"Fair enough, but I've been thinking a lot about it and realizing I should have pushed for more discussion about all this stuff earlier. And he said he's been trying to talk to me about the New Hampshire house for a while. Maybe he's right. It's exactly the sort of thing I wouldn't want to hear so I could imagine cutting him off if he brought it up."

"Don't be too soft on him. You've waited a long time to start traveling. Look how long it's been since you were here in Paris, for instance. You've talked about it plenty of times with me, so I'm sure you also talked about it with him. He was obviously choosing not to listen either."

"Let's not talk about him. How do you think Kallie is? We've talked a couple of times on FaceTime, and she seems good."

"I think she's doing well. Her apartment is miniscule, but her roommate seems nice, and she had me cracking up at some of her disaster date stories." Angela looked hard at Jane. "How are you feeling about all of this now that you've had some time?"

"It's getting better. At first, I felt *so* betrayed. I lost all confidence in my ability to judge people. I mean—I had put all my love and all my trust into this relationship. How could I have misread him so badly?"

Angela squeezed her hand.

"But then I was incredibly angry. At him for making me question my own judgement, and also at him for blatantly ignoring what *I* needed. But also angry at myself for not asking more questions earlier. I mean—I knew I married a staunch New Englander. I knew he loved being close to home. Why did I ever feel he would change?"

"Wait. Don't put too much blame on yourself. Yes, he's a New Englander, and all that implies, but he married you, an Air Force brat who'd made very clear how much you loved traveling the world. I don't see any evidence he had that in mind at all. Selfish bastard."

Jane was silent for a long moment, then smiled. "Let's forget about him and focus on the now. I have so much to tell you which is why I was so glad when you said you were coming. Let's get you upstairs for a shower and to unpack."

Jane signaled to Sylvie for the check and Angela reached into her black and white Longchamp bag.

"Nope this is my treat," Jane insisted. "You can pay me back by listening and offering sage advice while you're here." They both grinned and Angela gave Jane another hug before grabbing the handle of her bright red bag to walk the short distance to the apartment.

"When's the last time you were here?" Jane asked as she opened the door.

"Two or three years ago." Angela walked into the living room and plopped down. "Ooh, this leather chair is new. I like it!" She pulled the handle on the side to lift a footrest up into position. "Nice."

"Do you want to take the second bedroom or join me in the queen bed?"

"I'll take the small room. Then I can spread my stuff out with no guilt." Angela grabbed her bag and rolled it through. "I'm ready for that shower, then let's take a walk so I can try to stay awake."

Thirty minutes later, her hair wound into a soft towel, Angela flopped back into the leather chair. "Ah, that's better. What do you have planned for us?"

"We'll head first to the Left Bank for lunch after a quick stop at the bookstore." At Angela's puzzled look, Jane smiled. "There are a couple of books I have to buy for my interview and test this Thursday."

"Interview? Test?"

"Yes, to get into professional cooking school."

Angela's mouth fell open. "What the hell? How is it I

know nothing about this new development?"

Jane laughed. "I'll give you the whole story over lunch, which you're buying me after we find the books I need. Get your clothes on, and let's get out of here."

An hour later they were seated at a table in the sun with two glasses of rosé in front of them.

"That was quick work at the bookstore. Let me see what you bought. Wait—these aren't cookbooks."

"No, they're actually reference books on restaurant terms that Véronique recommended."

Angela read aloud, "*Culinary Dictionary: English to French* and *Cartes & Menus de Restaurant: Dictionnaire francais-anglais'*. Oh, I see. Okay, it's time to fill me in."

After they'd ordered, Jane talked about her epiphany at Véronique's house and the process she'd gone through since including Véronique's email to the schools.

"How lucky that she was your partner at the cooking class."

"I know, right?"

"I certainly remember those early days in Boston when you would feed anyone and everyone at our apartment on the weekends. I always resented Jack for sweeping you off your feet and taking you away. I almost went bankrupt on takeout after that." Angela grinned just as the waiter arrived with their food.

"You think I should do it, then? Cooking school, I mean?"

"I like the idea. More importantly, what do *you* think?"

"I think that if I get accepted, I do want to give it a try." Jane paused, and her expression sobered. "But if I do stay and do it, what does that mean for me and Jack? How will he react? I'd have to be here for a few months. Would he come to visit?" She paused again. "Or maybe if I choose this, I'm actually also choosing divorce."

Angela looked at her but didn't say anything for a long moment. "And how do you feel about that?"

"I don't know. I do know it feels absolutely like the right choice to stay and do this."

"What about your current job? And what about after you have your training? Would you come back to Boston?"

"All very good questions. I haven't allowed my brain to think that far down the road. I had already been thinking about quitting as I thought about traveling more." She stopped abruptly. "I just don't know."

"And you don't need to know right now," Angela said quickly. "Sorry for even asking. Typical me trying to figure out all the answers right away."

"Véronique says I should get you to quiz me from these books while you're here. She also suggested we go to some of the new restaurants and take notes on dishes we try. She says our best bet is to try to get in at lunchtime when they're less crowded."

"So, you're asking me to taste food in cool, hip restaurants around Paris as part of our homework for the week? I think I can handle that."

Jane turned to catch the eye of the waiter. "Could we have two lemon tarts, please?"

Angela looked over at her.

"I think we should each have one to celebrate. They're delicious." Jane's eyes sparkled with mischief, and before she could say anymore, she heard a voice behind her.

"Madame has decided to taste our lemon tart once again?" Jane could feel her cheeks getting warm and she turned toward Bernard's smiling face.

"Yes, Chef." Jane turned back to Angela. "Angela, this

is Bernard..."

"Bernard Dubois." He reached out to warmly grasp Angela's hand. *"Enchanté."*

"Nice to meet you, too." Angela's look was calculating as her gaze went back and forth between the two of them.

"Bernard was the guest chef at our cooking class who made the *coq au vin*. And then I ran into him, completely by chance, at a bookstore and then here." Jane knew she was babbling, but she couldn't stop herself. "I hope you don't mind me stopping by again," she said, turning back to Bernard.

"Not at all. I'm glad I had the chance to meet your beautiful friend. Please enjoy your tart."

Bernard smiled at each of them before walking away. It took all of Jane's willpower to keep her eyes from following him. Angela waited until he was out of sight. "Ooh la la. Now *that* is what I'm talking about. You didn't mention *him* when you told me about the class."

Jane blushed and Angela continued. "And somehow, randomly, you brought me to his café for lunch?"

"Well, the food was good when I was here last time," Jane said, her eyes wide in mock innocence. "Now, eat your tart like a good girl and open up one of the books to a random page and start quizzing me."

Chapter 17

Jane and Angela ate at several of the restaurants on Véronique's list, and each time, they took pictures and asked a myriad of questions. They charmed the waiters with their genuine interest and enthusiasm, and even persuaded some of the chefs to explain particular dishes and techniques. They made one waiter blush at their effusive praise of his deboning skills on a beautiful trout almandine.

Each evening, Angela grilled Jane on the culinary terms in the dictionary while Jane honed her cooking skills, including trying to make the perfect omelet. They had animated discussions about the various foods they'd enjoyed, from duck confit to fish and meat dishes with a myriad of sauces. It was all accompanied by lots of laughter and many glasses of wine.

Jane had chosen *Le Chateaubriand*, which Bernard had mentioned at the bookstore, as their final destination. It was only open in the evenings, and in fact Jane had to break the news to Angela that morning she had only been able to get two spots for the second seating, which started at 10:30.

Angela was aghast. "10:30?" "Really?"

"Yep. People eat a lot later here, haven't you noticed?"

"Yeah, but that seems extreme. But whatever. You know I'm up for anything.

"There's a special surprise which will soften the agony."

"Really?" Angela looked intrigued. "Have you found me my own Bernard?"

"He's not *my* Bernard," Jane protested, but she refused to say anything more.

They arrived at the restaurant at 10:25, and the maître d' showed them to a table at the far end of the restaurant. A man was already seated, and as they got nearer, he rose and gave Jane a kiss on each cheek, grinning.

"Zis must be Angela?" His English was accented, his voice a pleasant baritone. Angela turned to look at Jane who was grinning.

"Angela, let me introduce my friend, Francois Mercier."

"Nice to meet you." Her eyes widened. "Not *the* Francois?"

"Yes." Jane laughed out loud. "That expression on her face is very rare, Francois. I almost never succeed in surprising her."

"You certainly did this time." Angela turned to Francois. "I know all about the time you two spent together back in college, and she said she'd found the bakery, but she did *not* say she'd found you."

Francois told Angela the story while the waiter got them champagne.

"Here's to reconnecting to old friends," Francois said.

"And making new ones," Angela added, clinking glasses with both of them.

The evening passed in a blur of delicious food courses

paired with delectable wines. The three of them agreed it was one of the best meals they'd ever had. Jane noticed several times through the evening that Francois and Angela seemed to be exchanging small glances and studying each other when the other wasn't looking. Could there be some attraction there? Jane loved the idea of these two people who she cared about, caring for each other. She'd have to grill Angela when they were alone.

Francois called an Uber and dropped them at the apartment, asking the car to wait as he kissed them goodbye. He said he was in town all week and made Jane promise she would let him know the moment she heard from the school.

Angela stumbled slightly as they climbed the stairs to the apartment, declaring loudly that restaurants in Boston should offer a late seating option, then tumbled into bed.

*****

Thursday morning arrived, and after breakfast at Sylvie's, who loved hearing all about their incredible meal, Jane set off, feeling jittery but excited. Twenty minutes ahead of her appointment, she stood across the street from the school, *École Langelier*, gathering her courage. Then, with head held high, she strode purposefully forward, striving for an air of self-confidence even while her heart hammered loudly in her ears.

The lobby seating area was minimalist and modern, with several stark wooden chairs and an uncomfortable-looking Scandinavian-style couch. A young woman behind a chrome and steel desk looked up as Jane entered, giving her a frank appraisal from behind a pair of bright purple glasses.

"*Bonjour, Madame.*"

"*Bonjour, Madame,*" Jane replied. "I have an

appointment at 11:00," she continued in French. The young woman motioned her over to a chair, and then, with a dismissive sniff, resumed reading her glossy magazine. Once seated, Jane dared to take a surreptitious look around, noticing, for the first time, a man seated across from her engrossed in a newspaper.

At the same moment she glanced over, the man lowered his paper, and with a shock, Jane found herself gazing into a familiar pair of intense, dark brown eyes.

"Bernard," Jane said, blushing. "What are you doing here?"

"Jane," Bernard said, rising to greet her, but before he could move forward, the receptionist beckoned for him to follow her, and with a shrug and an apologetic smile, he turned towards the door the receptionist held open. His well-worn blue jeans once again hugged his hips, and this time, instead of a chef coat, he wore a neatly pressed, navy button-down shirt that was tucked in over a flat stomach. Jane tried not to stare, but her eyes, like the rest of her body, seemed to have acquired a mind of their own.

As he reached back to close the door behind him, he smiled at her and gave one of his Gallic shrugs. His bold gaze was frankly admiring, and her heart, which she'd just managed to bring back under control, began to beat rapidly again.

Shortly thereafter, the receptionist beckoned to Jane, and her heart started hammering again as she was directed into an empty classroom. As Véronique had predicted, she was asked to cook an omelet—a deceptively simple task, as she knew well from the many cooking shows she'd watched. She fumbled slightly in her nervousness, taking extra time to pick out the pan to use, and then taking several minutes to figure out how to operate the stove top. However, in the end, she placed a smooth, light-yellow omelet onto the waiting plate, and felt a small surge of satisfaction.

Next, she was handed a short, written assessment, defining various culinary terms and cooking techniques. The instructor told her to try to answer in French, and she was pleasantly surprised to find she knew all but a couple of the terms. The work she and Angela had done together had definitely paid off. She left the building feeling both exhausted and exhilarated, and sent texts to Véronique, Fiona, and Francois, promising to let them all know when she heard anything.

As she rode back to the apartment, she texted Angela to say she was on her way. She kept going over her performance and the exam, critiquing herself on what she should have done differently.

Her mind moved on to Bernard. Why had he been there? Was he taking an advanced class? Or was he there applying for a job? The questions looped endlessly through her brain, and she tried, in vain, to banish them completely.

All afternoon, she felt restless and unable to settle, and Angela finally lost patience with her, suggesting they take a long walk. In her nervousness, she'd forgotten to ask when she could expect her test results. Now she felt too sheepish to call, remembering the haughty receptionist.

By the following day, she'd not heard anything and was convinced she'd failed. She kept trying to mentally prepare herself, but her heart still pounded whenever she opened her email. Angela suggested they distract themselves with an afternoon showing of *All About Eve* at the Christine 21, another theater Jane had visited often as a student. She texted Francois and he sent a smiling emoji, saying he was sorry he had to work instead of joining them, but to let him know where they ended up afterward.

Emerging into the late afternoon sun, Jane almost fainted when she opened her phone to find an email saying she'd done well on the tests, and that Chef Alain was pleased to welcome her to the program, which would start the following Monday.

She and Angela hopped up and down in the middle of the street, causing a small traffic jam.

"We have to celebrate!" Angela announced, and she led the way to a small café nearby where she ordered champagne.

"This drinking champagne is becoming a regular habit," Jane said, smiling.

After raising their glasses, Angela asked for more details, and Jane opened the email again. "There's a list of things I have to buy at a store called Dehillerin over on the Right Bank. I can do that tomorrow when you leave for the airport."

She texted Francois and he promised to come right over. She then sent texts to Fiona and Véronique, who sent ecstatic replies, promising to raise a glass when they all saw each other in London.

For a brief moment, her giddiness was replaced by unease. She would have to talk to Jack. Soon.

But not tonight.

Chapter 18

As Jane stood under the hot shower the next morning, she winced slightly, knowing the water beating down would not be enough to soothe her pounding head. Angela had insisted they follow dinner with a stop at a bar and a dance club, telling anyone who would listen (many did not) that her friend was going to be a famous chef. At one point, while Francois was in the restroom, Angela went on and on about how hot he was, and how sorry she was to be leaving the next day. Jane remembered vaguely getting into the Uber but didn't remember much about actually arriving at the apartment.

Jane went in the kitchen and downed a huge glass of water with aspirin before going to wake Angela. She stood in the bedroom doorway for a moment before it sank in that Angela wasn't there, and that her bed was still made. She smiled to herself. It looked like her observations at the restaurant had been correct. She opened her phone and found a text waiting for her.

Meet me at Sylvie's in an hour? And please order me a LARGE café crème. 😊

When Angela arrived, Jane handed her two aspirin which she downed immediately.

"Well, well," Jane said, her gaze intense.

Angela had the grace to look abashed. "It was not planned, believe me." She then smiled. "But I'm not sorry it happened."

"I'm not sorry either." Jane said.

"Really? You promise you're not interested in him anymore?"

"I'm not interested. He's all yours. I told you—we're just friends."

"Okay." Angela said, looking relieved. She took a large sip of her coffee. "Do you remember us putting you in the Uber about 1 AM?"

"Vaguely. *Why* did you order that bottle of champagne at the last bar?"

"Because I'm an idiot?"

Jane tried to look disapproving, but they both burst out laughing. Sylvie looked over from the bar area and shook her head.

"I can't believe you're leaving me today," sighed Jane.

"I can't believe it either. Especially after meeting Francois."

"'Meeting.' Interesting choice of words," Jane said wryly. "Does this mean you'll be back soon to visit?"

"It's certainly tempting, but we've got a big pitch to a chain of high-end hotels in two weeks so I'm going to be slammed getting ready."

"How's the furniture business doing?"

"Really well, actually. But I don't want to talk about that. I'd rather talk about Francois. What a great guy! He's so easy to talk to. And cute. Especially those glasses. Sexy intellectual, you know?"

"So, was this a one-night stand or…?"

"Who knows at this point? I do know I had a great time, and I'd love to see him again."

"Did you two talk about that?"

"A little. He said he's always wanted to visit Boston, and this gives him the perfect excuse." Angela grinned.

"That sounds promising. Well, I'll grill him when he's in town next. What time is your flight?"

Angela sighed. "One o'clock, so I guess I need to go up and get packed."

Too soon, it was time to say goodbye. Jane gave Angela a fierce hug and then waved as the taxi pulled away. Opening her phone to find the email with the Dehillerin equipment list, she saw there was a text from Jack.

We need to talk.

She felt a moment of panic. Did he know about the school? No, he couldn't. Angela wouldn't have told him and no one else knew. What could it be, then? A confession about Barbara, maybe? Could be. Or something to do with Kallie? No, Angela said she was doing fine.

Having run through the immediate possibilities, and satisfied herself it couldn't be urgent, she pushed it from her mind. Her priority right now was preparing herself for starting class on Monday. Anything else had to take a back seat.

Chapter 19

Jane jumped out of bed, a glance outside showing a sky filled with dark gray clouds, but she couldn't stop smiling. It was her first day of school and she felt like a kid again, her stomach filled with butterflies of excitement and nervousness. As she showered, she mentally ran through her schedule—two classes each morning and one each afternoon except Friday, when she had the afternoon off. Her 'whites'—her sets of aprons and her chef's jacket—would be provided the first day of class.

After a quick breakfast, she packed her new knife roll, a water bottle, some snacks, and her wallet into her bag and set off for the school.

At the building entrance, she took a moment to take a selfie, feeling sheepish, but wanted to memorialize the moment. She double-checked the room number then set off, hoping her confident stride would convince her knotted stomach that all was well. That she could do this.

The receptionist motioned her through, and she joined others in front of the elevators. Were they all French or would there be others who spoke English?

The room looked identical to the one where she'd taken her test. Several ovens and stove tops were positioned at the far end of the room, while directly in front of her stretched a long metal table containing ten individual work stations. About half were already filled and she chose an open spot halfway up on one side.

She placed her things underneath the table on the shelf provided, then took one of the aprons and the chef's jacket from the counter and put both on, feeling self-conscious.

The young woman to her right had bright red hair and a large tattoo on her left arm. She grinned and stuck out her hand.

"*Salut. Je m'appelle Martine.*"

"*Je m'appelle Jane.*"

The chef entered the room, and everyone snapped to attention. Jane noticed the space next to her was still empty, but just before the doors were closed, there was a commotion and someone came to take the spot. "*Excusez-moi, Chef,*" he said, thrusting his things under the table as the chef began speaking.

"*Bonjour,* everyone. My name is Chef Sébastien. Welcome to our program. Any serious course in cooking must begin with an understanding of, and expertise with, knives. This class will teach you the best use for each of your knives as well as give you plenty of practice exercises to make you proficient. Please pull out your thirteen-centimeter knife."

Jane reached down and opened her new knife roll, searching for the right one. She glanced, for the first time, at the man who had arrived next to her. His knife roll looked creased and well-used.

"Hello, Jane."

"Bernard. Hello." She couldn't believe it. What was he doing in this class? She felt a moment of panic. She couldn't possibly be in the same class as him. He already worked as a chef. Flustered, she turned her attention quickly to the front of the room.

"Please pay attention everyone," intoned the Chef. He spoke only in French, but generally he spoke clearly and slowly, so Jane was able to follow along. It was only if he lapsed into a more conversational tone that she missed certain phrases.

Jane tried to not let herself be distracted by Bernard but couldn't help noticing how at ease he was. He finished each exercise more quickly and neatly than anyone else. The Chef had noticed, too.

Well, why wouldn't he finish first? She thought irritably. *He's already a chef.*

Chef Sébastien usually waited after each instruction to allow time for the English-speaking tutor to repeat it, but occasionally, if he was intent on making a particular point, he would forget. After one particularly rapid set of instructions, a quiet voice near her left ear said, in English, "He wants you to be sure to avoid cutting off the end of the onion, so that when you make the vertical slices, it will not fall apart." Startled, Jane turned and found an amused pair of brown eyes six inches from her own.

"*M-Merci,*" she stammered. His hands reached over and gently changed the position of the onion in her hands.

After twenty more minutes of concentrating on making slices and then working to cut those into small identical squares, they took a short break, and Jane wiped her hands on her apron.

"How are you doing?" Bernard asked.

"Fine." Jane's response was curt, and she didn't look at him, pretending to look for something in her leather bag. She finally added grudgingly, "Thank you for your help."

"You are welcome."

Looking over at him finally, she couldn't keep the irritation out of her voice. "You do realize you're showing the rest of us up, right? If it's not too personal a question, why are you in this class?"

Bernard at first looked taken aback at her tone, but then was apologetic. "I'm sorry you feel that way. The short answer is I was at the point in my career where I needed more formal training, and this school requires you to take *every* course in the curriculum to receive a *diplôme*, even if you have some of the training already."

"Oh." His explanation did make sense, though it didn't make his proficiency any less annoying. "Sorry I snapped at you."

"What about you?"

"Me? What do you mean?"

"If it's not too personal a question, why are *you* in this class? This seems like a big step up from taking a one-day cooking class for tourists." He was smiling, but his voice was mocking.

"The short answer is tourist classes like that won't get me where I want to go." Did that make her sound full of herself? She flushed, uncomfortable.

He was quiet for a long moment, then replied, "Good for you for recognizing that."

"*Attention,*" growled the Chef, and there was no more time to talk. She and Martine began to compare notes, while directing occasional questions to Bernard, and by the end of the ninety minutes, Jane felt she'd made a new friend.

As she finished putting away her knives, Bernard spoke up just behind her, startling her. "What other classes do you have today?"

"My next one is on kitchen hygiene, and then I have

one at three o'clock on pastry basics."

"I have one now on roasting techniques, then I'm also in the pastry class. Want to meet in the lobby after this next one to get something to eat?"

She tried to keep the surprise out of her voice. "I'd like that."

"See you at 1:15."

Jane hurried to her next class and tried to pay attention, but a lecture on kitchen hygiene, especially one in French, couldn't compete with musings about the upcoming lunch. Finally, it was time to go, and she hurried down to the lobby.

She found Bernard sitting on one of the benches, checking his phone, and he looked up and smiled as soon as she turned the corner. She couldn't help it—that smile made her heart do flip flops.

A little breathless, Jane said, "Do you know a good place to eat nearby?"

His smile became mischievous. "Yes, I do, as a matter of fact. Let's go."

Out on the street, he walked over to the parking area and stopped next to a motorcycle. He opened the compartment at the back and pulled out two helmets.

"It's just a short ride."

She hesitated, then took the proffered helmet.

At first, she was tentative in her grasp around his waist but after a couple of swerves to avoid rumbling buses, she tightened her grip. Ten minutes later, he pulled into a space between two parked cars, and Jane realized, with a start of recognition, they were arriving at the café where he worked, but from behind.

"*Salut, Bernard.* What are you doing here? You are not working today." The waiter approached and shook Bernard's hand vigorously. After he'd seated them, and gone to fetch silverware and menus, a burly, gray-haired man hurried over, greeting Bernard warmly, and asking questions in a quick torrent of heavily accented French. Jane was pleased she understood most of Bernard's side of the conversation at least.

When there was a pause, Bernard turned toward Jane and introduced her. "Jane, this is the owner, Maurice Leblanc. He's a very close friend of my uncle. Maurice, this is Jane." Maurice shook her hand and made a quiet comment to Bernard who laughed, looking embarrassed.

After he'd walked away, Jane said, "I admit I couldn't follow much of what he was saying."

"He said you're beautiful and I shouldn't let you get away," Bernard explained. The slow smile that followed made her stomach tighten.

She worked to keep her tone light. "But you told him I'm just one of the other students, right?"

"That doesn't matter to him. He's formed his opinion, and nothing I say will change that. The reason he was hard to understand is he's from Marseille. That southern accent has a definite twang."

"I was guessing somewhere south."

"According to him, everyone and everything is better down there." He smiled. "He's the one who told me to find a school and get my *diplôme*. He's taught me a lot, but he thinks I need more formal training to live up to my potential." For a moment he looked sheepish.

"That's a nice endorsement." They were both quiet as the waiter set down their food. "When we had coffee, you said you're from Dijon. Were you a chef there?"

"No, believe it or not I was a teacher at a *lycée*. The equivalent of your high school." He laughed at her look of surprise.

"Really? How in the world did you end up here?"

Bernard didn't answer for a long moment and when he spoke his voice was quiet. "I lost my wife, and I decided to start over with something completely different." He looked so sad that Jane reached out to touch his hand.

"I am so sorry."

"Thank you. It was a big shock." She thought he would stop there, but after a moment he continued. "She had ovarian cancer, so it happened very quickly." For a moment he looked surprised at his own revelation.

There was nothing Jane could think of to say. After a moment, she asked, "Did you meet in Dijon?"

"Yes. Christine was from London and on a wine study course. After we got married, we moved to London for a couple of years, but once we had our son, we moved back to Dijon to be close to my parents, and because we missed the food and wine." He laughed at her look. "I know what you're thinking. London has good restaurants, right? That's true, but not compared with France."

Jane laughed. "Nothing like confidence in your country's cuisine."

He started to protest, and she raised her hand. "I'm just giving you a hard time. I haven't spent enough time in London to have an opinion on that, but I'll take your word for it." Jane found herself noticing once more the golden suns surrounding his pupils, and to distract herself, she busied herself with her food. "So, you have a son?"

"Yes, Antoine. He and his wife live in Dijon."

"Oh, what does he do there?"

"He is a *négociant* – that is, he negotiates on behalf of a consolidated group of small vineyards to get them the best price for their grapes."

Over coffee, Jane told him about Kallie and her new

job in New York. "I'm looking forward to going up there to see her when I'm back in the States."

"You haven't mentioned your husband. Is he going to join you here while you do the cooking course?"

Jane looked uncomfortable. "Um, no."

He raised an eyebrow, but sat quietly, not pressing, and she liked him all the more for that.

"It's complicated. There's stuff going on and I needed to get away to think things through."

"*D'accord.*" "Okay."

"I'd rather not talk about it, if you don't mind."

"Let's talk about something else, then. How did you like the classes today?"

"Very much," she said, relieved to be on safer ground. "I think this is going to be a really good program for me. What about for you? Will the classes be challenging enough?"

"I think so. Some will end up as practice of things I already know, that's true, but there will be new skills and techniques as well. And to advance in this career, as I said, having the *diplôme* is helpful."

"Do you think you'll stay in Paris after you finish?"

"I have no idea. There are certainly lots of opportunities here. *On verra.* We shall see."

"I could imagine it would be nice for you to go back to Dijon."

"Maybe. I left there two months after Christine died and I don't know how it would feel to be there without her. Her death made me take a hard look at my life and that's when I realized what I enjoyed most wasn't teaching, but cooking. I'd only ever done it as a hobby, for friends and family, but I found it relaxing."

"Me, too."

"At school there were always new crises—sometimes

administrative and sometimes with unmotivated students and their demanding parents—but solutions were never clear-cut. I hated always waiting for others to weigh in and feeling like things were out of my control. It's not like that in the kitchen."

Jane leaned forward. "That's exactly how I feel at my job. Every year more and more paperwork and less and less actual teaching and mentoring. An anonymous committee who have the final say on my curriculum. No autonomy and no control. To escape, I head home and immerse myself in some new recipe where I can be creative and do things my way. It's what's kept me sane."

"Cooking in a restaurant isn't always creative, unfortunately. Sometimes, I think I'll go crazy if I make one more croque monsieur, but you're right. It's the creative side that keeps me coming back every day."

"I assume like the addition of the thyme to your delicious lemon tart."

He nodded, looking pleased.

"It must have been hard to leave Dijon behind, though."

"It was hard. I miss my family, but I couldn't escape the sadness there. Here, the city is full of activity, full of new people and new experiences. Like this class. And meeting you."

Jane met his intense gaze for a moment, then looked out toward the street, feeling her face flush. "Your friends must have thought you were crazy to move away."

"They did. To leave a teaching job with a pension and start over in a new career at forty-five. Completely *dingue*. Crazy."

"A month ago, I probably would have agreed with them, but I'm starting to see how unexpected changes in your life might lead to something better. How instead of being scared or sad, maybe I need to lean into it. See where it leads."

Bernard gazed at her for a long moment before gently touching his wine glass to hers. "Let's toast to drastic changes. We've arrived at this moment from very different starting places, but I'm happy we ended up at the same spot."

She held his gaze, feeling her pulse quicken. "Me, too."

On the metro ride home, she opened her phone briefly, noting with a mixture of guilt and relief there were no new texts or emails from Jack.

Chapter 20

Jane and Martine quickly became inseparable, helping each other with difficult dishes and reassuring each other when the chef teachers seemed overly critical. It was Martine who suggested they get together in the evenings to practice the techniques and recipes they'd learned, but the apartment she shared with her drummer boyfriend, Julien, and their two chihuahuas was tiny, so Jane offered Bobbie's apartment instead. The arrangement suited both women very well: Martine liked the company because Julien was away most evenings; and Jane was finding the evenings too quiet since Angela had left.

Martine had invited Bernard to join them as well, ostensibly for his practical knowledge, though she teased Jane about her obvious interest in him. His work schedule didn't give him much free time, so Martine and Jane were both surprised that he tried to be there most nights. The days he had morning classes, he worked the lunch shift at the café, so was not always able to stop by, but when he did, he'd offer last-minute advice and then share whatever dish she and Martine had prepared. If he had class all day, he would come with them to the apartment afterward and there was much laughter and jostling as the three vied for space in the small kitchen. Jane had never felt so exhausted, nor felt so fulfilled.

*****

"Dammit," Jane muttered under her breath.

"That is not French," came the amused reply next to her. She looked over at Bernard, who was smiling at her in sympathy. "What's going on?"

Jane replied in English. "My *beurre blanc* sauce has broken. It's the second time I've tried. Why won't it work?" She looked furtively across the room to be sure Chef Sébastien hadn't heard.

"Give me a minute," he said, whisking his own sauce while Jane cleaned out her saucepan. His sauce, of course, was perfect. "Okay, show me what you did."

She set her saucepan on the burner again, acutely aware of him as he stood close behind her to watch. His warm breath tickled her neck as he looked over her shoulder.

Willing herself to stay focused, she said, "Okay, I'm putting in the shallots and white wine and vinegar to simmer. Right?"

"Yes, exactly. Now we wait for a moment, to let it reduce a little." Bernard did not move away as they watched in silence, and Jane had to fight the urge to relax back against his solid chest.

After a couple of minutes, Jane continued, "Now I add cream and salt. And then I can start adding the butter…"

"Wait!" Startled, Jane lifted her wooden spoon. Bernard reached over to touch the butter she'd sliced and set next to the oven. "These are too warm. Go to the *frigo*—the fridge—you need cold butter."

She scurried to the fridge and back.

"Okay, now cut it quickly into small pieces and add them very slowly, one at a time, while whisking. Turn the heat down slightly, too."

She started whisking slowly, adding the butter only when Bernard told her to. A few minutes later, a beautifully textured sauce slid gently off her spoon. Smiling, she turned and for a moment, their eyes locked, but her gaze faltered as she noticed the Chef step up behind him.

"*Bonjour, Chef,*" Jane said, stepping aside. Chef Sébastien lifted her spoon from the pan. After a moment, he grunted, "It's good, well done."

"*Merci, Chef.*" As he moved away, Jane realized she'd been holding her breath. She and Bernard shared a conspiratorial smile of victory.

*****

"What shall we make tonight, *Madame*?" Bernard asked as they made their way to the street.

"Well, I obviously need to practice that *beurre blanc* sauce again."

"Then let's see if we can find some fresh fish. I'm sorry Martine wasn't feeling well. I guess you'll have to depend on me as your sous chef."

"Yeah, right. I think you have that backwards."

At the fishmonger, Bernard chose a couple of whole fish, discussing the various choices with the grizzled man who ran the stand. Jane watched and listened carefully, noting the varieties she didn't recognize to look up when they got back to the apartment. Their next stop was the vegetable stand, where they picked out green beans and the makings for a green salad. "Potatoes?" Bernard asked.

"No need. I have some small yellow ones at home." Their final stop was for a fresh baguette.

Back at the apartment, they set to work, Jane preparing the potatoes and the *haricot verts*, and Bernard in charge of fileting the fish. They worked in companionable silence, moving around each other in the small kitchen to find what they needed. Just before they sat down, Jane made the *beurre blanc*, with Bernard standing nearby to oversee her efforts. She was very aware of the slightly musky smell of his aftershave.

Once they were seated, Jane closed her eyes for her first bite, the soft flesh of the fish offering a slightly briny flavor, complemented by the lemony sauce. As they ate, they discussed the tastes and the textures of each dish, and she realized how much she loved having in-depth conversations about food, something she would never have even considered with Jack or Angela. Bernard cared as much about the flavors and cooking as she did, and always added insights based on his own experiences.

Jane set down her fork, sighing with contentment. "We did well."

"I agree." Bernard smiled his slow smile. "Your sauce tonight is delicious. Do you understand now why you had trouble earlier?"

"Not really."

"A *beurre blanc*, like mayonnaise and vinaigrette, is an emulsion, which means it's a fat that is being suspended in water. Since fat and water don't mix, emulsified sauces are always on the verge of separating like yours did today."

"Okay, so far that makes sense. So how do you keep it from separating?"

"You make the droplets of the mixture finer by whisking them quickly, and then you add an ingredient that will act as a bridge to hold it all together. In this case, that was the cold butter pieces."

"I'm still not sure why mine broke."

"Ah, because the *other* critical element is the temperature while all of this is going on. Too much heat makes the butterfat separate, so the butter has to be very cold. Yours had been out next to the stove for too long." Bernard suddenly looked embarrassed. "Sorry, that's probably way more detail than you'd ever want. What can I say? I like the science behind the cooking."

"I can tell," Jane teased. "But I do appreciate knowing why it didn't work. And I can see why you were a good teacher."

"*Merci, Madame.*"

She found his gaze a bit disconcerting and, feeling flustered, she rose to take the plates to the kitchen. She motioned for him to stay seated when he started to get up to help.

"I'll just be a second. You'll be proud of me—I pulled the cheese out of the fridge when we started dinner to bring it to room temperature."

"*Bon.* You're learning." Jane pretended to look outraged but couldn't help smiling as she headed out to the kitchen. "Don't forget the bread," he said to her retreating back.

Noticing their wine glasses needed refilling, Bernard stood and strode quickly toward the kitchen to retrieve the bottle. Jane was just returning, cheese plate in one hand, and breadbasket in the other, and they found themselves nose to nose in the narrow hallway.

For a moment, they stood stock-still, then Bernard bent down, his kiss lightly brushing Jane's lips. Jane moved instinctively toward him, hampered by having both hands full, and he deepened the kiss, his hand gently cradling her neck.

Jane felt herself leaning in even further, opening her mouth willingly. No more thought, only sensation. She let herself drown in the taste and smell of him.

She pulled back first, opening her eyes and gazing into Bernard's. "Wow," she whispered.

Bernard smiled. "As you say. Wow. I was just going to get us more wine."

They simultaneously moved to the right, then to the left. Bernard, laughing, gently held Jane in place, and slipped past. Jane continued to the table, setting everything down, then stood for a moment, her hand on her thudding heart.

She heard Bernard returning and plopped down into her chair. He refilled their glasses before taking his own seat. His dark eyes seemed to drink her in, and he reached for her right hand. "I've wanted to do that since...well, since that first time I saw you in Jacques' cooking class."

"No, you haven't."

"Yes, I have. I called Jacques that night to ask how the class went, but really to find out about you."

"Really?"

"He wouldn't tell me anything except your name, so I told him I would give him a note to forward to you. Before I could even do that, I saw you at the bookstore, and then at the café, so that just made me more determined to get in touch. When I saw you at *École Langelier*, it felt like Fate was throwing us together."

She noticed how full his lips were, and that the bottom one stuck out slightly.

He leaned toward her again, and she pulled back reluctantly, though she left her hand in his.

"I can't. Things are complicated right now."

"Can we talk about it?"

She hesitated for only a moment before it all came spilling out. About the disastrous evening and Jack's pronouncement. "I haven't spoken to him since. He did text me a couple of days ago saying we need to talk, but I've been ignoring it."

She looked sheepish when he raised an eyebrow. "I'm not ready," she protested. "I'll have to tell him I've started this course, for instance, and he's going to freak out about that. About me committing to something that will keep me here for months."

Bernard nodded but didn't say anything.

"And at this point, I don't even know what's going to happen with this course. If I'll stick with it or decide I can't handle it. So why tell him and subject myself to all his drama?"

"Do you think he would come join you if you told him you need to stay for a while?"

She was silent for a long moment before whispering, "I'm not sure I want him here."

"Ah. I can see why you said it's complicated. Let me ask it another way. Do you miss him?"

"If I'm honest, not really. I'm lonely sometimes, but I think maybe that's just because I'm used to having someone around. When I try to imagine him *here*, I just can't see it. He'd be unhappy with the language he doesn't understand, some of the foods, and especially not having a car.... It's a very different life here."

"It sounds like you do have some things to work through. Okay. I will try to be patient." The look in his eyes belied his tone, and she was surprised by her own sudden intense longing.

"I think that's best." She hoped her own quickened heartbeat and breathless tone were not as obvious to him as they felt to her.

Chapter 21

Jane struggled out of sleep. Something was buzzing next to her ear, and her fuzzy brain finally realized it was her phone. She glanced at the clock next to the bed. 4:30 AM? What the hell?

Normally, she turned her phone to silent mode at midnight since she was in a different time zone from friends and family in the States, but the previous night she'd forgotten.

She picked up the phone. It was Jack's number. That made her heart start thumping.

"Hello? Hello? Jack?"

"Jane? Thank God I reached you. Sorry, I know it's the middle of the night for you. Kallie's in the hospital."

"What?"

"She's okay, she's okay. She's at Mass General."

"What? She's with you? Why isn't she in New York? What's going on?"

"She came up for the weekend and started complaining about a bad stomach ache. We thought it was the clams we'd eaten, but it just kept getting worse, and when she couldn't stand up straight, I took her to the emergency room. It turns out she has acute appendicitis. Thank God we have such great medical care so close. They immediately took her in for surgery, and I'm waiting to hear."

"Oh my God." Jane was now fully awake and already calculating how she could miss class and get a flight to Boston as quickly as possible.

"I'm sorry I couldn't call earlier, but once I decided to bring her in, there was no time."

"No, I completely understand. I'll start looking at flights."

"No, don't do anything yet. Let me find out what the story is on her recovery and I'll call you back."

"Okay. I won't be able to go back to sleep, so call me as soon as you know more. Thank God tomorrow—I mean today—is Sunday, so I don't have class. Call me as soon as you hear, okay?"

"Of course, I promise. She should be out in a couple of hours."

*****

Two hours later, the phone buzzed again, and Jane picked it up immediately. She'd tried to go back to sleep, but her swirling thoughts kept taking disastrous turns, so she'd given up and was sitting at her dining table, sipping coffee and bookmarking a couple of flight options.

"Jack? How is she?"

"She's fine. Dr. Graves said it was very inflamed, so she was glad we came in when we did before it burst."

"Thank God."

"She can go home in a day or two, but then she can't go back to work for another week, so I'm trying to persuade her to stay here for that time."

"Absolutely. Then you can make sure she's eating right and not doing too much."

"That's what I thought, too." Jane could hear the hesitation in his voice when he spoke again. "Do you think you'll come back to see her?"

"Of course. I've already found a couple of possible flights."

"Great. She'll feel better if you're here."

Jane suddenly realized that since Jack didn't know she'd started at the school, he would assume she had infinite flexibility in terms of staying in Boston through Kallie's recovery, but now wasn't the time to get into all that. "When would she then go back to New York?"

"I would say next week sometime."

"Okay, I'll text you my itinerary as soon as I have it."

"That sounds good." He hesitated before adding quietly, "I hope this gives us a chance to chat a little, too. You got my text?"

"Um, yes."

"I do need to talk to you. It will be better in person."

"Okay." She was afraid to say anything more and risk starting a longer conversation. He was right. Whatever it was he wanted to say would be better in person.

"Give Kallie a hug for me and tell her I'll be home soon." Jane hung up, and since it was after midnight in Boston, texted Angela instead of calling her. She also texted Martine and Bernard that she'd had a family emergency and to give a call when they were awake.

She finalized her flight reservation and when she put it in her calendar, she realized she'd miss Veronique's store opening in London. She knew Véronique and Fiona would understand but she felt a pang of disappointment.

When Angela called, she sounded horrified. "Oh my God, I'm so glad she was home with Jack. That was a lucky break."

"Absolutely." For a brief moment Jane let herself imagine Kallie, instead, in her apartment alone.

"I got your itinerary and I'm happy to pick you up. I assume you'll stay with me here?"

"Yes please, though I'm going to ask Jack if I can stay at the house the first couple of days to be near Kallie, even if it's a bit weird."

"How did he sound?"

"A little freaked out the first time we talked, but much calmer the second time. He said he's glad we'll have a chance to talk in person."

"That's interesting. Do you think he'll tell you about Barbara?"

"That's what I'm thinking."

"He's got to assume you've seen them on Facebook."

"Maybe, but he isn't on any social media himself and is generally pretty clueless about all that stuff."

"Well, Barbara certainly likes posting pictures. Okay, I'll see you outside baggage claim on Tuesday. Can't wait to see you."

"Thanks again. Love you and see you then."

Chapter 22

"I can't believe you're here!" Kallie was propped up on multiple pillows, and Jane hugged her, taking care not to squeeze too hard.

"Don't I get some credit for bringing her?" asked Angela, who was standing just behind Jane, waiting her turn.

Kallie tried to laugh, but grimaced instead, holding her stomach. "Ouch, please don't make me laugh. I'm glad you're both here."

"It doesn't seem completely real, to be honest," said Jane, rubbing her eyes. "I didn't sleep much on the plane, so this is all feeling a little like a dream." She gazed around Kallie's room, smiling fondly at the various high school and college trophies and mementos.

"This place is overflowing with flowers. How many friends do you have anyway?" Angela asked as she moved baskets off the two chairs to make room for them to both sit down.

Kallie made a face. "They're mostly from Dad's friends and business associates."

"Well, I'd say you're spoiled rotten." Angela grinned

at Kallie for a moment, then said, "I need some coffee. Anyone else want some? Jane, I know you do."

"Yes, please. Kallie?"

"I'd love some green tea."

"One coffee, one green tea coming up. I'll see what I can find to eat as well." Angela saluted and left the room, giving Jane a pointed look. Angela had been pressing Jane on the drive over to take advantage of this unexpected opportunity of being face to face with Kallie to have a frank discussion about her real reason for running off to Paris.

Jane helped adjust Kallie's various pillows, then pulled the chair up close to the bed.

"How are you really feeling?"

"Good. Sore, but good."

"I'm so glad you were here instead of New York. And speaking of that, why were you here?"

"I came down to confront Dad. As soon as I heard you and Angela were in Paris, I knew something was up. You've been talking to me for months about surprising him with a trip to Paris after I left for New York, so I asked him about it on the phone. He came up with some lame excuse about deals at work keeping him here, but I didn't believe that. He's always bragging about his great team so why couldn't they handle things? I decided I need to confront him in person."

Jane watched Kallie's face closely. "And what did he say?"

"At first, he still said it was because of work, but after I told him that was crap, he finally admitted that you two were 'sorting through some things' and that you'd decided to go without him. Is that true?"

Jane wrestled with herself over how much to say. "That's true in essence, but there's more to the story." She was interrupted by Angela's return carrying a tray with two steaming plates and cups.

"I've brought omelets that I think will be okay. I watched your mom when she was making them for us in Paris, so I figured I'd give it a try."

Kallie's voice was strained. "I'm sure it will be delicious. Thanks, Aunt Angie."

"I'll leave you two to it and go take my work call. Yell if you need anything."

They ate in silence for a moment, then Jane spoke again. "The day you left for New York, your Dad and I started discussing our future and it quickly became apparent that we were worlds apart." She reached into her bag and brought out the crumpled ball that had been the travel list, handing it to Kallie.

Kallie unfolded it carefully, then was silent as she studied it.

Paris- Michelin star, farm to table

Normandy/Brittany- Moules/frites, crepes

Madrid- Manchego, Iberico, tortilla española

Rome- pasta with truffle

Tokyo- ramen, gyoza, sushi

New Zealand- lamb, red wine

London- curry, fish and chips, Michelin star

Thailand- panang, laab, spring rolls

Budapest- goulash, paprikash

"What is this?"

"A list we made on our honeymoon of all the places we'd visit when we had the money and time."

"You were already obsessed with food I see," Kallie said smiling.

Jane laughed. "What can I say? It's a big part of who I am as you know.

"So, what happened?"

"It turned out he didn't even remember making the list. I was shocked. I've held on to that list all these years because I thought it represented a plan we'd made. A plan that one day he'd hand over the daily running of the business to that team he was bragging about to you, and we'd set off to see the world."

Jane was silent a long moment, then continued. "As you got older, I started to suggest places we could take you. He always had an excuse for why we couldn't go too far away or for too long. A deal he couldn't leave, or your various sports commitments." Jane held up her hand when Kallie opened her mouth to protest. "I didn't argue because they were legitimate excuses. So, each year we'd just do the same thing we'd always done. Spend time with family at the lake house in New Hampshire."

"I loved those vacations and I love that house," Kallie protested. "I remember how bummed I was the first year I went to girl scout camp and only got to spent August with the rest of you up there."

"They *were* great summers. I totally agree. But if I'd had a choice, we wouldn't have been there *every* summer. But that was how Jack was raised, and that's what he wanted you to grow up with, too."

"What's wrong with that?" Kallie's voice had risen.

"Nothing. Nothing at all," Jane said. "I loved it too, but spending *all* of my time in New England doesn't work for me, Kallie. It's never been enough. My choice would have been to expose you, when you were young, to other cultures, and travel to other countries, but he was very resistant, so finally I stopped pushing. Maybe I shouldn't have given up, but that's water under the bridge now."

Jane gazed out the window. "I thought he understood how important travel was to me, and how much I'd sacrificed by not doing it. Whenever I'd feel sad or frustrated, I'd pull out that list and remind myself that one day it would be different. But it turns out that wasn't true. At least not for him."

"So, what does that mean? You are coming back, right? You're just visiting there."

"I don't know what's going to happen."

Kallie's eyes filled. "You have a good life here."

"Yes, but if it's for the *rest* of my life, I'm not sure it's enough."

Kallie didn't say anything for a long moment. She stared down into her tea, moving the last piece of her toast around and around her plate in slow circles. "I do understand Paris was an important part of your life and I totally understand why you wanted to go back to visit favorite spots and relive old memories. But this is home."

At first, Jane couldn't speak past the lump in her throat. "Boston will always be special to me, but getting back to Paris has reminded me how special it is, too. It also reminded me how much I love cooking."

She took Kallie's hands. "I've started a professional cooking course that will keep me in Paris till the fall." At Kallie's look of shock, she added, "I know—it was not something I planned, but it feels right."

"But what about you and Dad?"

"I don't know. He wants something very different for his future. We'll talk about it again, but I'm not sure we can make it work." She looked over at Kallie and seeing the anguish on her face, she abruptly stood and left the room.

"Mom!" Kallie's voice followed her down the hallway,

but she stumbled down the stairs, moving blindly toward the kitchen she'd spent months designing and outfitting. She sank down onto one of the two café chairs she'd found at an antique shop in Boston. She lowered her head onto her arms, feeling completely spent. The sleepless flight, the stress of Kallie's illness, and finally the stress of being back in this house that looked exactly the same as when she'd left, were a heavy weight pulling her down, and she suddenly felt exhausted.

A hand gently touched her shoulder, and she looked up, startled, to find Jack standing next to her. Without a word, he held out a glass of wine, then beckoned toward the porch and its perfect view of the setting sun.

They settled into two Adirondack chairs facing the slowly darkening sky.

Jack spoke first. "One silver lining to Kallie's illness is that it brought you back here. I know we left things in a very bad place that night and I'd like to have the chance to finish the conversation."

"I thought you had finished it. You made very clear how you felt."

"There's something more that I didn't tell you."

"I know about Barbara, if that's your big reveal."

"You do?" Jack turned to face her, obviously shocked.

"Jack, you are so hopelessly naïve sometimes. Just because you don't use Facebook doesn't mean she doesn't. The photos Angela found of the two of you make it look like you're more than just work colleagues."

Jack was silent.

"So, what's the deal?"

"We did spend some time together after a couple of company events, but that's all it was." Jack turned to face Jane in the waning light. "Jane, you have to understand. I was feeling lonely and lost because Kallie was leaving, and you seemed more and more distant. It was stupid. I know that now. Barbara's interested in something more, but it made me realize I didn't want to lose what you and I have. I've been such an idiot. We don't have to get a divorce, do we?"

Now it was Jane's turn to remain silent.

"Being with her felt so easy," he continued. "She'd talk about growing up around here, and we'd laugh about places we'd been and things we'd done as kids. But the truth is, after a while, I realized it wasn't *easy*. It was *boring*. Jane, I like what we have. I like that we're different people, even if that means we disagree sometimes. It's a lot more interesting that way."

"This is more than a simple disagreement, Jack. This is the rest of our lives. Have your feelings about travelling changed?"

"Not really, but I'm willing to talk about it and come up with a plan that we can both agree to."

"That sounds *kind of* like a concession, but a really vague one that'll never amount to anything." Jane couldn't keep the sarcasm out of her voice.

"I'm sorry. That didn't come out right. I would be *happy* to travel with you—to Paris and to other places. I'm ready to figure out when and how."

"Wow. I never thought I'd hear you say that."

"Me, neither."

"Let me ask you a different question, then. Do you still see your retirement years being spent in New Hampshire?"

"Yes, but what if we just used that as our base and did trips to the places you want to go from there?"

"I don't think that would work. Did you notice you just said places 'you' want to go, not places 'we' want to go? Before long, you'd be finding excuses for not coming along on those trips, and I'd get more and more frustrated."

"I don't know about that. I understand now how important it is for you. Can you at least consider it?"

"I don't know. It may be too late." She paused, then said, "I've got something to tell you. I've started a professional cooking course."

"You've what?" Jack's voice rose. "How much time will that take? You haven't even been away a month. How could you make such a crazy decision?"

"A crazy decision? Crazier than buying a retirement property because it felt right? Well, this feels right to me."

"That's ridiculous."

"Because it's my idea and not yours? Because it's what *I* want?"

"No because what I did was just buy some land. You're talking about a much bigger commitment. Do you even have the cooking skills or the level of French language you need?"

Jane didn't want his comment to hurt, but it did. "Thank you *so* much for your vote of confidence." Her voice had also risen, and she suddenly remembered Angela was sitting in the next room. She tried to calm herself.

"That's not how I meant it, but do you?"

"Yes, I do." She made herself say it with conviction. He didn't need to know she'd been asking herself the same question.

"And how much time are we talking? Months? Years?"

"If I do the basic level, it's a minimum of three months."

"Three months?" His voice was incredulous.

"Yes, Jack. And longer if I decide to work toward the higher diploma. As you may recall, when I left here, I was under the assumption that we were getting divorced."

Jack shut his mouth suddenly, his face beet red, then snapped, "What about your job?"

"I'm going to quit." As she said it, she realized the decision had been made subconsciously even though she hadn't acknowledged it to herself.

"Just like that. Walk out on people who depend on you."

"Jack, I'm not having this conversation with you. I'm just starting to figure out what *I* want, and your pronouncement that night took away any rights you had to being part of that decision. I'm in Boston this week to help Kallie in her recovery. After that I'm going back to Paris. When I make my final decision about my future, I will let you know."

Angela had just appeared at the door, and Jane grabbed her purse and strode out, slamming the front door shut behind her.

Chapter 23

Since Fiona's return from Paris, summer had arrived in Liverpool, and it was helping her hang onto the happiness she'd found in the City of Light. Her first task upon her return had been the emotional process of cleaning out her mum's house, so manned with mops, brooms, and a cheerful playlist, she headed over her first weekend back. It had been sitting vacant for a year, since her mother's departure for the nursing home, and it looked drab and sad. A layer of dust covered every surface, and once she'd removed the covers from the furniture, she did a quick inventory to see what she could salvage. She separated out dishes and knickknacks she thought Kevin might like for the condo he'd moved into after his divorce, as well as the things she wanted to take to her own apartment, then put anything remaining into a large rummage sale pile, only keeping out things she felt would be useful for staging the house for sale.

She went online and ordered a furniture removal pick up, then bought a few small bits of inexpensive furniture and lamps for the staging. She bought a new duvet for the master bedroom in a bright French Provencal pattern, then browsed through potential paint colors thinking that if she could find someone who would do the work at a reasonable price, it would be a relatively inexpensive way to refresh the whole interior.

Next on her agenda was dealing with her own appearance. She had felt like such a different person in Paris—confident, attractive, even adventurous in her eating. Arriving home she'd fallen back into her old patterns but was determined to change. Her conversations with Emily provided good inspiration and she even had a time deadline because they'd made plans to meet in London for Véronique's store opening. After scouring reviews of the local hair salons online, she took an extended lunch break one day to visit a salon on the High Street with great reviews, Divine Do's by Manuelle. He'd ushered her in, fawning over her and exclaiming at how thick her hair was, and how much he loved her curls. When she left ninety minutes later, she couldn't believe the transformation from plain to—dare she say it—chic? She was sure she'd never remember his detailed instructions for how to style it herself.

Manuelle insisted her next step should be a visit to one of his favorite boutiques, La Femme Fatale, just across the street, to buy clothing to match her new and beautiful hair. She'd stood outside the shop feeling both fascinated and appalled in equal measure by the outfits on the mannequins. She couldn't imagine wearing anything she could see from her position on the sidewalk. Everything seemed either low cut, or skintight.

But she was determined to at least give it a try and pushed open the door, emerging forty minutes later with two large bags, exhilarated and new best friends with her salesperson, Nancy.

Nacy had then insisted she had to shop for new

lingerie, and though she'd blushed furiously throughout, she'd gone to a specialty shop and bought the first bras and panties she'd ever owned that weren't plain white from Marks & Spencer.

Newly self-confident in her appearance, she decided to join a French club and had already attended a couple of the get-togethers, speaking very little but feeling braver each time. She'd also reached out to several women from her business course and was gratified when they immediately suggested putting a date on the calendar to visit an exhibit at a local art gallery with lunch afterward.

The one happy hour after work she attended was a disaster. It was painfully obvious that no one was interested in her stories about Paris. One of the women in her department pulled her aside afterward to let her know that the other women thought she'd become 'a bit of a snob' since going away on holiday.

She couldn't wait for the London opening. She'd found an Airbnb to rent, and Emily had confirmed she would catch the afternoon train and meet Fiona at Bon Gout itself. Emily had apologized in advance that she could only stay the one night because of work obligations, but Fiona was thankful she could come at all. The only sad news had been from Jane who would be missing the event entirely, but Fiona promised to return soon to Paris so Jane could cook for her.

Saturday dawned clear and bright, and after an uneventful train trip and with the help of her London A to Z street map, Fiona found her way to the flat, which was sparsely furnished, but clean and comfortable.

As she headed back out, she took a quick look at her reflection in the mirror next to the front door. She'd gotten better at blow-drying her hair and the soft curls gently framed her face. She'd also put on a bit of makeup. Looking at her outfit, she had to smile, realizing the black trousers and crisp white blouse reflected Jane and Véronique's influence on her sense of style. The only difference was substituting black ballet flats for the high heeled boots they both favored. For a final pop of color, she added her Paris scarf and set off.

Bon Gout's storefront looked bright and inviting, and Fiona remembered Véronique saying how much she'd enjoyed working on the window displays. Their sense of style and playfulness reminded her of Véronique herself. On the left, oranges were stacked to look like a miniature volcano, with boxes of raspberries at the top representing the fiery center. Fresh herbs and varieties of salad greens made up the "fields" surrounding it. When she drew closer, Fiona discovered there were also small toy people with carts and farm tools. The tableau made her smile.

In the display on the right, wines and cheeses were grouped by region, and a colorful map behind them showed their geographic locations, as well as a short description of the wines themselves.

Just inside the main entrance, to the left, was a long table filled with name badges that looked like decorated macaron cookies, each with the store logo in one corner and the person's name in script in the center.

Véronique stood greeting the guests as they arrived, looking beautiful, though Fiona noticed she seemed uneasy, and her eyes kept glancing to one side as if she were looking for someone. Her face lit up when she saw Fiona, and she walked over to bring Fiona her name badge, kissing her warmly on each cheek.

"*Salut*," she said brightly. "I am *so* glad you were able to come!" She gave Fiona an approving look. "And you look beautiful. *Très chic.*"

Fiona ducked her head—embarrassed but pleased.

"Véronique, the store is absolutely perfect. Wonderfully inviting."

"Do you really think so? I have been working on it so long that I don't think I'm objective anymore."

"It's brilliant. And I *love* your display windows. They beckoned me inside."

"*Merci beaucoup.*" Véronique's smile faltered for a moment.

"Is everything okay?"

"Yes, I'm sure it will all be fine." She leaned in and whispered, "The main shipment of meats and cheeses didn't arrive yesterday, so we are trying to find out where it is. I'm sorry to be distracted."

"I totally understand. Well, I can tell you from this vantage point it all looks perfect." Fiona squeezed Veronique's arm reassuringly just as a group approached, smiling and holding glasses of champagne. "I'll leave you to it."

Fiona set off through the produce area—marveling at how fresh everything looked—then turned down a prepared food aisle and Fiona saw foie gras, duck confit, and the pork rillettes Véronique had served them at dinner. She liked the fact that items she'd rarely, if ever, seen in British grocery stores, were stacked next to mainstays like baked beans and jars of tomato sauce.

At the back of the store were two large display cases that Fiona assumed must be where the fresh meat and cheese should be. They were currently covered by brightly painted cloths, one of cows in a sunlit pasture, and the other of a traditional farmhouse and bright red barn.

Poor Véronique. Fiona glanced at her watch and saw it was just 5:00 so there was still time for the shipment to arrive before most of the guests, but she could certainly understand Véronique's concern. Behind the cases, an area had been curtained off, and there were people in chef's outfits opening jars and cans and filling trays of food that waiters were then taking to hand out.

Canapés, she thought with a smile.

As she gazed back along the way she'd come, she marveled at all that Véronique had accomplished. This was so much more complicated than what she dealt with at the factory. Her mind buzzed with ideas and questions.

Fiona suddenly realized she could hear murmuring coming toward her, but from the next aisle over, and as they approached, the words became clearer.

"They have done a good job of bringing in a variety of new and different products." The haughty British voice sounded approving, but then a second voice cut in, the heavy French accent almost sickly sweet. "Yes, I agree, though it's too bad about the late shipments."

The voices rounded the corner and Fiona turned quickly toward the shelves, making a show of reading a label while she listened. The two women glanced over and lowered their voices slightly, and Fiona had to crane her neck to overhear them. The older British woman was dressed in a suit that Fiona was sure was St John, its crisp lines hugging the woman's slim figure. She wore large diamond earrings and black pumps with a ubiquitous gold Ferragamo buckle on the top. Her haughty demeanor and the young woman's fawning posture made it evident she was 'somebody' or at least, she thought she was. Fiona instantly disliked them both. The younger woman's bright red nails were making wide sweeps in the air as she continued talking.

"Yes, it really is a shame. We are still waiting for the large shipment to arrive. I can't imagine what happened."

Could this woman be the evil Camille from Véronique's office? Fiona wondered. If so, the fact she was spouting on about the shipment to someone who looked important was bad. Very bad. Fiona made a show of finishing her review of the label and walked past the two, trying in her quick glance to read the woman's name tag.

"Sylvia Something," she murmured to herself.

Her phone buzzed and it was a text from Emily saying she was waiting outside. Fiona hurried to the front of the store and found her next to the entrance, looking beautiful in light grey slacks and a yellow blouse. They hugged tightly, then Emily stepped back and gave Fiona an appraising stare. "You look really good."

Fiona blushed. "Thank you."

"Let's go see this fancy store. I'm dying to meet everyone after hearing so much about them."

"I told you Jane isn't here, right?" Fiona asked as they went to find Emily's name badge. About half of the badges were now gone.

"Yes, I'm sorry I won't get to meet her, but hopefully we can go back to Paris soon and I can see her then."

"That's exactly what I told her," Fiona said, and they shared a smile.

"Hasn't Véronique done a marvelous job?" Fiona said loudly as she glanced around them, then added under her breath, "We need to find her. I overheard a conversation she'll want to know about. Some behind-the-scenes drama."

Emily looked concerned. "Oh no. What about?"

Fiona explained about the late shipments. "We need to ask someone on the staff who that woman is, then report back to Véronique as soon as we can." Fiona approached a young woman issuing instructions to several waiters. "Excuse me, I wonder if you can help me. I am looking for a woman that my friend told me would be here tonight. Sylvia....?"

"Oh, Sylvia Sinclair? Oh, yes, she arrived about

twenty minutes ago."

"Great, thank you so much." Fiona took Emily's arm and led her down an aisle toward the back of the store. "Quick. Look her up on your phone. Who's Sylvia Sinclair?"

After a moment of tapping, Emily crowed, "Well, well, she is a well-known writer and reviewer for Time Out magazine. Impressive that they got her to come to the opening."

"Let's go find Véronique. Oh, I hope the shipment came in or is on its way!"

They threaded their way through the now crowded aisles until Fiona caught a glimpse of the top of Véronique's head. She was in the wine section, chatting with Jean-Pierre and another young man.

They started to move in that direction, but Fiona saw Véronique break away and head toward the small podium. At the same time, she noticed the waiters were handing out champagne flutes to anyone who didn't have one, and refilling those that did. The crowd quieted and Véronique tapped the side of her glass for attention.

"Thank you all for coming to the opening of our first store in London. We at Bon Gout pride ourselves on the quality of our products, and we hope we can provide you with foods you love as well as new foods to try. I hope you will come back soon—and please bring all your friends." There was scattered laughter. Raising her glass, she added, "I want to raise a toast to my wonderful staff who have worked so hard these past weeks." She raised her glass, and everyone did the same. "And a toast to our wonderful President for his vision and willingness to take a chance on something completely new." She nodded at Jean Gauthier, who raised his glass in acknowledgement as the crowd cheered. "Now, please continue to enjoy the food and champagne."

Loud applause followed her as she made her way to where Fiona and Emily were now standing, next to Jean-Pierre and the other young man. Jean-Pierre kissed her and Fiona overheard him whisper "Well done, *ma chérie.*"

"Now that my official duties are done, I can really enjoy this glass," she answered, clinking glasses with each of them and then turned to Fiona. "Fiona, I want to introduce you and your friend to David, our website designer."

"Nice to meet you, David. And I want to introduce all of you to my friend, Emily. Emily, this is Jean-Pierre, and Véronique. David, you did a great job on the website, by the way."

Everyone shook hands, and David said, "Thank you. I am so proud of our whole team, and of course our esteemed leader, Véronique." He made a courtly bow to Véronique who punched him lightly on the arm. "Stop that!"

"You obviously did a good job getting the word out to the expat community," Fiona said. "I've heard quite a bit of French spoken. Now you just have to be sure they all bring their British friends. Should be easy with such delicious foods."

"*Merci*, Fiona."

Fiona lowered her voice. "Véronique, can we talk privately for just a moment?" She pulled Véronique slightly away and told her about the conversation she'd overheard.

"*Merde.* Yes, that was definitely Camille. She'll just make everything worse. Damn it! I'm worried. There's been no more news of the shipment." They rejoined the others but had only just started chatting when a voice sounded behind them.

"Excuse me for interrupting."

Véronique turned. "Monsieur Mercier. How nice to see you." She turned back. "Everyone, this is Monsieur Mercier, who oversees the baked goods division."

Francois nodded quickly at the group. "Nice to meet you all. Excuse me, but I must borrow Madame Moreau for a moment." He took her arm and led her away, and Véronique shot a nervous glance at Fiona.

Chapter 24

Francois' firm grip on her elbow was making Véronique's heart pound and her mouth dry. His voice was quiet as he spoke into her ear. "It would seem we have a small problem."

He led her through the crowd, smiling and nodding to people as they made their way toward the back of the store. She could see up ahead of them the curtained area and the waiters moving in with empty trays and out again with full ones. Next to the curtain stood two official-looking men.

"Good evening, gentlemen," Francois moved forward to shake their hands. "How can we help you?"

"Who's in charge here?" The first man was balding and slightly overweight, his buttons straining across a stomach that spoke of regular visits to the pub.

Francois motioned toward Véronique who was standing a half step behind him, urging her forward. "Madame Moreau oversees this store. And you are?"

The two men showed their badges. "We're from the Port Health Authority."

Véronique shook their hands. "What can we help you

with, sirs?" She was shocked by how calm she sounded.

"We have paperwork for a shipment that I believe you are expecting." The larger man thrust a set of stapled pages at Véronique. She glanced through them, then nodded. "Yes, we expected it yesterday."

"Do you have a copy of the pre-notification notice and confirmation for this shipment that you could share with us?"

Véronique's mind raced. The last week had been a blur of last-minute questions and paperwork. Did she have that? "Um, I am sure we do."

"Please go and fetch it, then. There is no record of any such notice in our files."

Véronique hurried away and entered her office, dismayed at the scattering of papers across the desk. She was normally a very organized person, but things had gotten out of control in the last forty-eight hours. She rummaged through the stacks to find the folder related to the import paperwork, then quickly leafed through it. Nothing.

She went through the remaining stacks, every second feeling like an hour. Nothing.

Taking a deep breath, she grabbed the import folder and hurried back to where the men, and Francois, were standing.

"I'm sorry, but I don't see it here. I'm sure we did send notice to your office."

"I'm sorry, madam, but as you know, if you have not provided notice in a timely manner, your shipment can be confiscated or even destroyed."

"No!" The cry was inadvertent and she quickly added, "I'm sorry. Things have been very hectic, but I am sure the paperwork was completed, and I can provide it to you. Please do not destroy our cargo."

"We will hold it for twenty-four hours awaiting your

confirmation paperwork. Please remember that you also need proof of the phytosanitary certificate which I also do not see here."

Véronique opened the folder and leafed through quickly, pulling out a paper triumphantly. "I do have that, sir. Here is the copy."

The two men took their time inspecting the paper, and Véronique's heart raced. Finally, the first man handed it back with a grudging, "That looks in order, madam."

The second man, who had not said a word, now spoke, his voice surprisingly deep. He was physically the opposite of his companion; wraithlike, with small glasses perched on his long, narrow nose. "Madam, are all of your permits for opening this establishment in order?"

"Yes, I had Inspector Stanley in this morning giving us our final review before opening for business."

He nodded gravely. "Ah, good man, Stanley. Very well. Please be sure the pre-notification paperwork is submitted immediately."

"Can we expect to then get our delivery on Monday?" Véronique had a sudden vision of the large containers of meat and cheese sitting for days in a warm warehouse.

"If the forms are submitted this evening, I would expect delivery could occur by Tuesday."

"Thank you, sir. I will take care of it right away. Thank you."

The men shook their hands once more, and Francois led them unobtrusively down a side aisle empty of clients and out a side door. Véronique could hear the murmur of his voice then a bark of laughter from the two men as they walked away.

David hurried up to Véronique, Jean-Pierre close behind. "What is it? What's happened?"

Jean-Pierre enfolded her in his arms. "I'm sure you will solve whatever it is."

For a moment Véronique couldn't speak. "A minor disaster that could still become a major disaster but is hopefully averted. I have to go get some paperwork submitted." She smiled tremulously, and Jean-Pierre tightened his arm around her.

"Are you sure you're okay?" David's face was creased with worry.

Véronique looked gratefully at the two men. "With the two of you behind me, how could I not succeed?"

"What can I do?" David asked.

"Can you please go find Claude and send him back here so I can let him know?" Her face fell. "By the way, Camille has been at it again." She quickly told them what Fiona had shared. "This *will* become a major disaster if Ms. Sinclair writes something nasty about us. After you find Claude, David, could you go find Camille and Ms. Sinclair? After you charm Ms. Sinclair, can you pull Camille aside and give her a piece of your mind? Does she not understand that we are all on the same team here?"

David shook his head in disgust. "You're right. She's gone too far this time. I can't believe her. I'll go find Claude then go find them. Don't worry." He hurried away and Jean-Pierre followed her into the office, not saying anything but smiling from his seat across from her. His mere presence calmed her and she opened her computer, scrolling through a myriad of emails, but not finding any evidence she'd sent the notification.

She sighed. "Looks like I did screw up. I'll be here for a while getting this form submitted. Would you mind going to find Fiona and her friend and tell them I'll be busy for a bit? And then do you want to head back to the hotel?"

Jean-Pierre shook his head. "No, I'm not going to abandon you. I will go and let them know, but then I'll come back here. I'm so sorry this happened, *ma chérie*, but you'll figure it all out." He gave her a quick kiss and left, closing the door quietly behind him.

A moment later the door opened again, and Francois stuck his head through. His normally cheerful smile was gone, replaced by a stern grimace. "Do you have things under control?"

"Yes, Monsieur Mercier. I will take care of everything."

"I'll leave you to it, then. We'll talk more back at the office when you return."

Chapter 25

After Fiona and Emily arrived back at the apartment, Emily opened one of the bottles of wine she'd bought at the store and poured them each a glass. Joining Fiona on the couch, she handed her one, tapping it gently. "Penny for your thoughts."

"I can't stop thinking about poor Véronique. She looked absolutely crushed."

"I can certainly understand why, though she shouldn't be. Yes, the forgotten form was an issue, but she got it submitted and hopefully has averted the potential disaster. Just as important was how she handled it. If you were one of the regular guests tonight, you would not have known anything was amiss."

"That's true."

"Of course, it's true. It's like a concert where the performer berates himself afterward for all the mistakes he's made, but no one in the audience noticed a thing."

"What if she can't get her shipment delivered and the food is all ruined?"

"Then she'll deal with it. It's obvious she's a very

competent young woman."

Fiona sighed, and Emily slid over to lean against her, pulling Fiona's arm around her and tucking her head against Fiona's shoulder. They sat together in silence for several moments. "I'm confident things will all be sorted next week," Emily murmured.

"I hope so. I just wanted it to be perfect for her."

"It will be—next time." Emily lifted her head to look at Fiona. "She did a fabulous job."

Fiona smiled. "She really did. When I was walking the aisles, I admit I was a bit envious. I'd love to work on something like that."

"Maybe you could get in touch with that Claude fellow and ask him to give you a tour of all the back operations. You're such a nerd, you'd love it."

Fiona set her glass down and turned to wrap both her arms around Emily. "How do you already know me so well?"

"Figuring that out wasn't hard. No one else would have asked him all those questions. I felt sorry for the poor man." Emily snuggled closer.

Fiona smiled into Emily's hair. "You're right. I did get a little carried away. I'm so glad you got to meet everybody, by the way. We need to go back to Paris soon so you can meet Jane, too. It's funny how close I feel to them both after just a week together."

"It doesn't always take a lot of time if you just click with someone. Look at us. I'm just someone you met at a café." Emily glanced up and they both smiled. She snuggled back in. "How are things going with your Mum's house?"

Fiona filled her in with the latest updates, then talked about how being there had been painful, but also cathartic. How it had brought back all the frustration of losing her mother mentally long before she lost her physically. "To see someone who had been my support for so many years gradually become a lesser version of herself was so hard. We did have a wonderful conversation on her last evening, when she seemed almost her old self again, and I will always be grateful for that."

Emily sat back so she could look at Fiona. "That was a wonderful gift. It's funny how often you hear stories like that. Where it seems like you're given one final chance to say goodbye."

They sat in silence for a moment longer then Emily stood, stretching. "I'm exhausted. I was in budget meetings at the university today and there will be more tomorrow. Let's get some sleep."

By unspoken consent they pushed the two twin beds closer together and Fiona sat on the edge of one, motioning for Emily to sit down opposite her. Taking her hands, Fiona said, "I am so happy we met, but I need to tell you that I'm nervous, too. This has never happened to me before. The way I feel about you. Whatever this is, or this becomes, I need to go slowly."

"I understand."

Emily's green eyes regarded her intently, filled with warmth, and suddenly, despite what she'd just said, Fiona wanted Emily to kiss her like she had that last night in Paris. She leaned forward, at first tentative then more firmly. They kissed for a long moment, and when they separated, Fiona smiled. "I reserve the right to change my mind. About that going slowly part."

"Okay. Duly noted." Emily smiled. "Like now?"

"No, but maybe soon."

Once they were both tucked in, Emily reached across to take Fiona's hand. "Thank you. For being at the café that day, and for reminding me that sometimes taking risks can be worth the rewards." She squeezed Fiona's hand, then released it to reach up to turn out the light.

Fiona closed her eyes and briefly let herself imagine starting a new and different life in London. She would reach out to Claude Bernier. She smiled to herself, thinking about Emily's teasing.

Turning over, she listened for a moment to Emily's soft breathing, and wrapped in a sudden, unexpected, contentment, Fiona fell into a deep sleep.

Chapter 26

Salut! I'm on my way back. See u in class on Monday!

Jane finished typing and set her phone aside, glancing at the time. It was 10:30 in Paris so Martine might still respond before Jane had to switch off her phone for takeoff. When she'd texted Bernard earlier, he'd warned her that Chef Alain, the school administrator, had just been asking when she was due back.

She felt guilty for a moment for being away so long, but knew she'd needed to come back for her own peace of mind as well as to support Kallie. At the last minute, she'd also decided to accompany Kallie back to New York which had given her the chance to see Kallie's apartment, to meet her roommate, and most importantly, to continue the conversation about what the future held.

After her conversation with Jack, she'd escaped back to Angela's for some serious self-reflection. In the end, she knew she still loved Jack, but the reality was that any future with him would be full of compromises she had realized she didn't want to make. It was time to face the facts and admit to herself and to him that divorce was inevitable.

She would go back to Paris and continue her culinary journey. She knew it would be exhausting, but also exhilarating, and wherever it took her in the future, for the moment it was giving her a sense of accomplishment and fulfillment.

Her phone dinged, bringing her out of her reverie. It was Martine. In French, she'd written:

Can't wait to see you. Julien's playing at a club in the 20th next week. Want to come?

Jane quickly typed back:

Maybe. Let's see how jet lagged I am. Glad tomorrow is Sunday so I can recover a little before class.
Can't wait to see you.

After an uneventful flight, Jane could feel herself relaxing as soon as she opened the apartment door. It felt like home. She looked around the now familiar entryway and walked through the living room to open the shutters. First priority was a shower. She grabbed fresh clothes and stood under the steaming jets for as long as she could stand it.

Next up was food. In her rush to go see Kallie in Boston, she hadn't emptied the fridge, so she now went through and pulled out some spoiled strawberries and a yellowed head of broccoli to dispose of on her way to the grocery. Grabbing the largest canvas bag, she had a moment of déjà vu of her first morning that made her smile, then grabbed her keys and purse and opened the door.

Bernard stood there, his hand raised, frozen in the act of knocking.

She stopped, her heart pounding. He looked good.

Tired, with a slight stubble on his chin, but with that sparkle in his eyes. And that smile. Oh, that sexy smile.

"*Bonjour*. Welcome back."

She smiled back. "What are you doing here? You're supposed to be sleeping. Isn't that what you usually do on your day off?"

"It is, but I decided you needed a proper meal your first day back."

"Well, in that case, would you care to join me in my grocery shopping trip?"

"With pleasure, Madame."

They descended the stairs and as they walked to the various shops, Jane felt her senses were heightened, the sights smells, and sounds assaulting her. The damp aroma of the wet pavement, the warm smell of garlic from the Italian restaurant they passed, the acrid plume of bus exhaust as it roared by. The flowers in the window boxes were a profusion of color that almost hurt her eyes—reds, and purples, and yellows. Even the quality of the light itself—making the silhouettes of the buildings more stark, making the sky a more piercing blue. And underneath it all, the constant buzz of traffic, even on this quiet Sunday, broken by the occasional sharp blast of a horn or siren. She didn't know if it was because of the jet lag, or Bernard's presence but the city felt vibrant, and alive.

She was also very conscious of each small interaction with Bernard—the fleeting pressure of his hand on her back as they descended the stairs, his hand brushing hers when they both reached for the same bottle of wine at the store.

Bernard chose two beautiful steaks at the butcher, and Jane enjoyed listening to the two men discuss the various cuts available, and the benefits and drawbacks to each. They moved next door where they picked out asparagus at the organic market, and ingredients to make a summer salad—

crisp green lettuce, juicy red tomatoes, and a small box of dried currants and nuts to add crunch and tartness. Next stop was the bakery where they found a gorgeous strawberry tart, the fruit glistening atop a golden crust.

Back at the apartment, Bernard took charge of creating the sauces, first a hollandaise for the asparagus, then starting again but this time adding shallots and tarragon to transform it into a bearnaise for the steak.

"I hope you realize how lucky you are. You get *two* sauces created by the famous Chef Bernard in one night," he teased, his eyes dancing.

She found enormous enjoyment in the familiar routine of preparing a meal together—the small tasks of cleaning and breaking the asparagus, the washing and cutting up of each element of the salad, the making of a simple vinaigrette to dress it.

She smiled at him, responding with her most obsequious tone. "Oh, I am so honored."

Bernard's eyes never left hers, and his slow smile made her heart begin to beat faster. She hurriedly turned away, busying herself with slicing the baguette.

When everything was ready, they carried their plates to the table, and Bernard poured them each some wine. She held the wine in her mouth for a moment. Notes of cherry? Or was it blackberry?

She took her first bite of the steak, closing her eyes to focus on the tang of the tarragon and the rich buttery taste of the bearnaise blending perfectly with the intense flavor of the rare steak. Next, she took a bite of the asparagus coated with the tart lemony hollandaise, and again closed her eyes to fully savor it.

Before coming to Paris, she'd eaten meals she would have described as delicious, but now, with her newly acquired knowledge of the techniques that developed those flavors to their fullest, it was as if a curtain had been pulled away. Each bite held layer upon layer of building richness, which was in turn heightened and changed with each sip of wine.

Jane opened her eyes and found Bernard watching her, smiling. Self-conscious, she took a quick sip. "What are you looking at?"

"I can almost see your brain and your taste buds having a discussion about each flavor, and I love it."

Jane blushed and Bernard's gaze became more intense. "Jane, do you know how beautiful you are right now? The way you close your eyes halfway, and lick your lips just slightly..."

He stood abruptly and pulled her to her feet, lowering his head to cover her mouth with his with a pressure that startled her with its intensity. She immediately wrapped her arms around his neck, her own pent-up desire overwhelming any last bit of restraint. After a long moment, he lifted his head and held her tightly against his chest.

His voice was choked and slightly muffled as he spoke into her hair. "I have been thinking about you every moment you've been away." He held her away from him so he could look into her eyes. "Kallie is fine?"

"Yes, and the extra couple of days with her in New York was wonderful."

"And.... with Jack?" Jane could feel how rigidly he held himself waiting for her answer.

"We are getting a divorce."

Bernard continued to hold her at arm's length. "And how do you feel about that?"

"It's what I want. I'll always love him, but I don't want to be married to him."

She looked up at him and the look in his eyes

emboldened her to add, "I missed you, and I missed the life I've started making for myself here."

Bernard gently caressed her cheek. "I've missed you, too."

She pulled his head down to kiss him again, and his arms tightened around her. Their kiss deepened, and she let herself drown in the sensations and the tastes, and she had a sudden intense longing to touch his skin. Her hands impatiently reached for the buttons on his shirt.

"*Ma chèrie....*" His voice was husky, and he picked her up, carrying her to the bedroom. His fingers gently caressed her wrist, before he bent to kiss the spot where his hand had been, sending electric shocks up her arm, and she groaned. Then he was kissing her lips again, and she stopped him just long enough to turn and fling back the covers. He started to undress her, gently kissing each bit of skin that he uncovered, and they fell backwards onto the bed, their kisses becoming more and more urgent, as he threw off his own clothes. They lay for a moment facing each other, and Jane ran her hand along the smooth line of his toned body, touching first his shoulder, sliding down to his waist, and on down to run along the curve of his thigh. Bernard lay still, smiling that incredible smile she couldn't resist, then moved towards her, taking away her breath as his mouth covered hers once more. She moaned as his hands and clever fingers caressed her, first gently, and then more and more urgently. She let herself drown in the many sensations, shutting out the rest of the world.

*****

"*Tu as faim?* Are you hungry?" a voice softly whispered in her ear.

Jane slowly opened her eyes to find Bernard propped on one elbow, his brown eyes slowly traveling down to where the sheet had slipped down off one of her shoulders. He reached over to gently cover her and to tuck a stray lock of hair behind her ear.

She was trying hard to not be distracted by his touch, or his twinkling eyes, when her stomach gave a loud growl. She blushed, but said defensively, "Why wouldn't I be hungry since I only had one bite of that delicious steak. What time is it?"

Midnight. Not too late for a light dinner?"

Jane reached for him, pulling him towards her for a lingering kiss. "Not too late at all. And that was a very effective technique for getting rid of my jet lag. Did you sleep?"

"A bit, but I couldn't stop looking at you." His gaze was intense.

How long had it been since Jack had looked at her like that? She glanced around at their clothes scattered on the floor and gestured with mock reproach. "We've made quite a mess."

"Ah, well, you know from cooking that sometimes you have to make a mess to create a work of art." He raised one eyebrow, and Jane giggled.

"Laying it on a little thick, don't you think?" Her eyes twinkled. "I'm starving. Where are my clothes?" She put her feet on the floor and grabbed the first thing she saw which was his shirt. "Can I wear this?"

"*Absolument.*" He rose, pulling on his jeans.

"I have an idea of something to cook for us, if you will allow me, Monsieur Chef," she said, grinning.

"I would love that." He motioned for her to precede him.

She took their plates to the kitchen and pulled out a skillet, the eggs, and some butter. "Steak and eggs. It's an American classic, *non?*"

Bernard laughed and nodded.

As she mixed the eggs and set the butter into the skillet to melt, it reminded her of making the omelet the day of her tests. She was feeling much more confident this time. Pulling a clean plate out, she touched the edges of the omelet with the spatula, then with a quick twist of her wrist, rolled it out onto the plate. It was a perfect pale yellow.

Bernard clapped. "*C'est magnifique.*"

"Monsieur, would you do me the honor of slicing us some baguette?"

She quickly reheated the steak and made another omelet for herself. They carried their plates out to the table, and Bernard retrieved their napkins from where they'd fallen on the floor.

With her first bite, Jane found herself focusing once again on the intense flavors of everything: the farm egg; the freshly ground salt and pepper; the meaty steak, and the crunch of the baguette crust.

Is this how good every meal will taste from now on? She couldn't believe how each experience brought new, sharp tastes.

They didn't speak, reveling in their mutual enjoyment of the simple meal, hearing an occasional car horn or shout of laughter from outside the open windows. They carried the dirty plates and glasses back to the kitchen, and as she rinsed them to put into the dishwasher, he stood behind her, encircling her with his arms. She leaned back into him, loving the feel of his solid chest. It felt exactly as she'd imagined it would.

She turned to face him, her soapy hands encircling his

neck. "*Merci, Bernard.* You make me feel"—she searched for a moment—"cherished."

"I'm glad. You deserve to feel cherished." He kissed her and after a long moment, he pulled away to murmur, "If you dry those cold, wet, hands of yours, I would love to prove it to you again."

She laughed and reached for the towel.

*****

The next time she woke was to bright sunshine and a clear, azure sky. She'd forgotten to close the shutters in the bedroom, and the sun's rays slanted directly down onto the bed. She glanced over to see Bernard still asleep, his curly hair a dark mop across his forehead. His mouth hung open slightly, and she smiled at the sound of his gentle snore.

She lay back, reliving each moment of the previous day and evening, then stretched, feeling as though she'd slept for a week. The clock on the side table said 6:30, so they had a couple of hours before class started.

She searched inside herself for regret but found only quiet joy. She turned again to look at him, and this time his dark brown eyes were open, a slight smile on his lips.

"*Bonjour.* Did you sleep well, *ma chèrie?*"

"Very."

He continued gazing at her, his hand moving to cup her breast before continuing to slide down, caressing her stomach as it moved ever downward. Her body arched to meet it.

"Ahhhhh...."

He smiled. "That's what I thought you would say." She noticed the slightly rough feel of his chin before the kiss deepened, and she let other sensations take over, emptying her mind once again of all thought.

*****

"Now we're going to be late and Chef Alain is already mad at me," Jane said, smiling, as she pulled her clothes on and ran a brush through her hair.

Bernard shrugged his Gallic shrug. "Was it not worth it?" then ducked away as she threw a pillow at him.

As Jane turned to lock the door behind them, she giggled.

"What's so funny?"

"I was just thinking about the nickname I gave you when I saw you for the first time at Jacques' class." She looked at him, giggling again.

"Yes?" He raised his eyebrow.

"*Monsieur Bedhead.*" She pushed past him, starting down the stairs. "Looks like my assessment was correct!"

As Bernard held the door for her to exit onto the street, he smiled his sexy smile. "I wish I'd known about that nickname sooner."

Chapter 27

Véronique kept glancing at her phone, willing the minutes to move more quickly. Nervously, she got up to get yet another coffee, then sat fidgeting and rearranging the items on her desk.

Monsieur Gauthier had emailed her the afternoon before, asking her to come to his office at 4:00 to meet with members of senior staff. She had just returned to Paris after staying over to oversee the delayed delivery of meat and cheese, which had fortunately arrived only slightly crushed and slightly warmer than would have been ideal.

There had been several other small glitches, but she was proud of the London team and how they'd all stepped up. She and Claude Bernier had met to go over what had gone well and what had failed, updating their outline of the permits and certificates and the timetable for each. Claude vowed to talk to the executive committee about hiring someone for future openings to oversee that process so he could focus on the physical construction issues, and she could have more time for the myriad of other puzzle pieces making up each project.

Véronique was relieved he wasn't angry at her for

missing the last crucial step in the pre-notification process, instead complimenting her on all she *had* accomplished, and she hoped he had expressed that same opinion to the members of the executive team. She'd know soon enough.

At 3:55, she made one more trip to the restroom to check her hair and makeup, and after a quick, critical look in the mirror, decided she was ready to face whatever was coming.

As she entered Monsieur Gauthier's office, he rose from his desk and motioned her toward the conference table, where she could see Francois Mercier and Claude Bernier already seated, as well as the head of Finance and the Director of HR.

"*Bonjour, messieurs dames,*" she said, perching stiffly on the edge of one of the conference room chairs. Claude was just across from her and gave her an encouraging wink.

"Now that you are back in Paris, we wanted to discuss the London opening in more detail."

"Yes, sir."

"Everyone here, as well as the members of the Board, were apprised of the problem with the delivery and felt you handled that situation with grace and professionalism. We are thankful you were able to keep the matter from becoming an issue for the people in attendance, and that members of the press were not informed."

"I am so sorry for the misstep, *Monsieur,*" Véronique murmured, her head down.

"It was a complicated project and we all learned from the missteps."

He paused, and the head of Finance spoke up. "The good news is the preliminary numbers are in, and the store is already doing very well," he said, breaking into a smile.

"My team has been working very hard." Véronique

said, and let herself relax ever so slightly into her seat.

"I also want to mention the article that came out in Time Out," Jean Gauthier spoke again. "Have you seen it?"

Véronique went rigid, feeling a moment of panic. She'd completely forgotten about the conversation Fiona had overheard between Camille and Sylvia Sinclair and in the week since then, she'd been so busy solving the various small crises she hadn't thought about it at all.

"I'm sorry to say I haven't seen the article." She looked directly at him, straightening her shoulders and bracing herself for the worst.

He picked up a copy of the magazine that was opened in front of him before continuing. "We were so pleased that Camille was able to persuade Sylvia Sinclair to attend, and frankly thought that would be the end of it. But in an article she wrote on the growing French expat community, she put in a very nice plug for the store, saying, and I quote, 'This tiny gem of a store provides an unexpected source for first quality products from France that, until now, have been difficult to find. Be sure to stop by to try their wonderful samples and to stock up before your next cocktail party.'"

Everyone was smiling, and with the relief flooding through her, Véronique suddenly had the urge to giggle hysterically. She swallowed hard to suppress it, gripping the chair arm.

Jean Gauthier continued. "Should the numbers remain strong for the next six to eight months, the Board has authorized me to consider a second London location. Though it's early days yet, I would love for you to take the lead on doing the initial research to decide that location, including the hiring of any outside consultants. Once the decision is made to move forward, you would, of course, then oversee the final project."

For a moment, she sat—stunned, thrilled, and terrified in equal measure. She'd spent the entire morning bracing for rejection, and this complete reversal was making her lightheaded. "Thank you for your confidence in me. I learned so much from this initial opening and would love the chance to put that knowledge into practice, however, I would like some time to think it over as well as discuss it with my husband."

"Absolutely. We will look forward to hearing from you soon and for myself, I hope you will agree to take this on."

Claude spoke up. "Véronique, Monsieur Gauthier and I have also spoken about the volume of paperwork and permitting we faced on this opening and the Board has agreed to allow me to hire a logistics person. Let's meet next week to discuss any ideas you have on that front."

"It would be my pleasure. Thank you all again for your confidence in me."

Véronique rose, still in a daze, and shook everyone's hands. She walked to the door, trying to keep her pace slow and steady instead of skipping across the room.

David was waiting at her desk, and she smiled hugely at him.

"Good news, then?"

"I can't believe it, but yes, *very* good news." She was about to say more when Camille rounded the corner.

"Véronique. I didn't know you were back." She slid her arm through David's and he looked at Véronique and rolled his eyes. "Sounds like quite a mess with that whole delivery debacle." Véronique thought Camille looked like a snake eyeing its prey.

"It all worked out fine," Véronique said airily, "A small delay, but the store is now well supplied and doing very well, thanks for asking." She shared a look with David before turning back to Camille. "Oh and thank you for inviting Sylvia Sinclair. The members of the Board are over the moon about her mention of the store in her article."

Camille's smile froze. "Uh, yes, I saw that. Good news."

"Very. You've helped me win the assignment to open the next store. I can't thank you enough."

Camille looked venomous for a brief moment before recovering her smile. "I'm so happy for you," she oozed before walking away, her stiff posture belying her tone.

"Well played," David said, laughing.

"Do you suppose she's learned her lesson?"

"What do you think?"

*****

Turning the lock on her apartment door, Véronique opened it to find Jean-Pierre standing by the stove, tomato sauce bubbling in front of him and steam rising from the large pot next to it.

"*Bonsoir, mon cheri*. What a wonderful surprise," she said, and he turned, smiling, his arms open wide. She moved into them, and he bent his head to hers for a long kiss.

He pulled away slowly, his arms still encircling her. "I'm sorry I've been so short these last weeks. Someone's always arguing over how to handle something and I'm always smoothing everyone's ruffled feathers. Tonight, on this new pitch, I told them all to grow up and figure it out for themselves. Then I walked out." He grinned. "It felt amazing."

"I'm the one who needs to say I'm sorry. I've been so wrapped up with my own problems and stresses I haven't paid any attention to all that you've been going through."

"Let's just agree it's been rough all around. Go get

changed and dinner should be just about ready when you get back."

When the steaming plates were in front of them, Véronique said, "I've got news. Monsieur Gauthier said that based on how well my store is already doing, he wants me to start researching a second London location." She watched Jean-Pierre's face carefully and her tone became defiant. "It wouldn't happen right away, of course, but if all goes well, it could start in six to eight months, and I would be in charge of overseeing the entire project again." She paused. "You know I'd like to do it."

Jean-Pierre was silent for a long moment, looking at her. "Of course I know that. And you would do a brilliant job, just as you did this time."

"Thank you for saying that."

"I hope you know how proud I am of you. You handled it all brilliantly, including the problems that came up."

"It means a lot to hear you say that."

"It's never been a question of whether you would succeed, Véronique. You are an incredibly talented and smart woman. It's a question of what we want for ourselves these next few years. Is our life going to continue like this, the two of us going from one stressful project to the next?"

"If I'm being honest, yes, I think so. It's what you have to do the first few years when you're trying to build a career."

Jean-Pierre sighed. "I don't want to agree, but I think you're right. Which brings up a related topic. The question of when to have kids. But on that subject, I have a confession to make."

"Yes?"

"Last weekend, watching David and Annette with Mathilde at her birthday party made me realize you're right.

Kids *are* a lot of work."

Véronique felt relieved. "I agree!"

"All that noise, and energy, and mess." Jean-Pierre grimaced. "I'm not ready for that yet."

Véronique smiled. "I totally agree. Let's focus on *us* for a couple more years before we add another little person or two to the mix. Okay?"

Jean-Pierre nodded.

"In the meantime," she continued, "let's be sure we take a moment, between those stressful projects, to reward ourselves. We'd talked about going away after the London opening, and your pitch to Vitesse, so let's do it."

"I'd love that."

"Good. I *might* have already started looking online when I got back to my office today." Jean-Pierre looked surprised then laughed loudly. She continued. "How does Brittany sound? Near the beach. Far from everyone and everything."

"That sounds perfect."

Chapter 28

Fiona gazed out the window, her thoughts moving forward with the gentle motion of the train's progress. She'd been surprised and pleased to hear from Claude Bernier, who asked if she would be interested in joining him at the weekly London store meeting on Sunday afternoon. He could answer her questions about general operations and she could meet the senior staff. She'd readily agreed and sent a note to Véronique thanking her profusely for passing on her contact information.

Chairs had been set up facing the same small podium that had been in place for the opening, but which now held an easel with a large pad of writing paper and pens. Claude began by letting them know Véronique was away for a few days on a well-deserved holiday. He then outlined the various glitches the night of the opening, starting with the near disaster of the delayed delivery, and then asked the staff to share their thoughts and critiques, with Rachel, the store manager, transcribing these onto the pad. Fiona was impressed with the staff's depth of knowledge of the various products as well as their frankness in describing the challenges they'd faced. She envied how easily they seemed to move from one language to the other.

"I want to congratulate you all on the store's tremendous success already," Claude continued. "Are there suggestions for things operationally we should be doing differently, now that you've been up and running?" There were several suggestions, and Fiona could see the camaraderie and supportive attitude they had for each other. She made a mental note to talk to Kevin about instituting a similar sort of update meeting at the factory.

"Finally, I have another bit of very good news. I've been told by the Board that if our sales numbers continue to show such promise, they are open to the idea of opening a second London location." There was applause and excited exclamations.

"Just to be clear, this won't happen right away, but I am happy to say that Véronique has been awarded the oversight of the project, and as part of her preliminary research, she'd love your ideas and thoughts."

Everyone started talking at once, throwing out possible locations, and also what criteria to consider when making the choice. When the meeting broke up, Fiona felt buoyed by the energy as various members of the staff shook her hand before making their way out of the room, still chatting.

Fiona and Claude walked to a nearby restaurant, and he listened with close interest to Fiona's thoughts on the various suggestions that had been made, both for the current operation and for the future locations.

As they sipped their coffees, he said, "Thank you for sharing your thoughts and your expertise with me. I know now I made mistakes in the permit and licensing process that cost us time and money and you seem to have exactly the sort of knowledge we need moving forward."

"I'm flattered you think so. The factory systems are much less complicated than your store operations."

"They may be less complicated, but I think with this sort of thing, the principles are the same."

He paused. "Véronique has shared with me a little of your story and let me say first I am very sorry for your recent loss."

"Thank you."

"I would imagine your brother needs you more than ever, so this is difficult for me to ask, but I would love for you to consider applying for this position."

"I don't know what to say except to say again I'm flattered."

"Véronique recommended you very highly."

"She is a very talented young woman and I would love to work with her and with your team, but as you say, I must also consider my brother and my current situation very carefully."

"I understand."

They finished their meal, and as they parted, Claude shook her hand. "I will forward the application when I am back at the office, which will include the salary specifics and some of the other details. I know we have only just met, but with Veronique's strong recommendation, and your interaction today with the staff, I am confident you would be a great addition to our team."

"Thank you so much. I promise I will think very seriously about it." She walked to the train station, her mind buzzing. Because she'd only ever worked at the factory, from summer jobs when she was young, to moving into her current role, she'd never actually had to apply for a job. What was an appropriate salary? She assumed she'd be based in London. How much did a flat cost?

But she was getting ahead of herself. She hadn't even applied, much less been offered a position. She couldn't wait to fill Emily in on how the day had gone, but also didn't want everyone on the train listening in. Once she was home, with a fresh cup of tea beside her, she would call.

Emily picked up on the first ring. "Tell me everything."

Fiona described the afternoon in detail, warmed by how interested Emily was in every aspect. "The staff is terrific, and I loved how comfortable they were in speaking frankly about the store and about the opening. I want to talk to Kevin about doing something similar here. I really felt it created some communal spirit and teamwork."

"I am assuming he didn't just invite you to answer questions. Is there a possible job opportunity like we hoped?"

"Yes. They are definitely looking for someone to join them to handle some of the logistics issues, and he basically offered it to me at lunch."

"That's fantastic!"

"It is, and what was especially meaningful to me was how respectful and sympathetic he was about losing my mum."

"I'm glad you got along so well."

"I really liked him. He's sending a link this evening to the application form and more details about the job itself."

"That all sounds great, but I don't hear as much excitement in your voice as I'd expected. You're worrying about Kevin, aren't you?"

Fiona felt herself choking up. "That's part of it for sure. If I leave, I will feel I'm abandoning him. But it's not just that. Emily, I don't know if I'm even qualified to talk to Claude. I've only ever worked at Braxton Blinds. I have no idea of the sorts of things he'd need me to know how to do.

How could I possibly be qualified for a job at such a large company?"

"We've talked about this." Emily's voice was soothing. "First off, you've been running the inventory, sales and delivery for an entire factory on your own, so of course you have expertise. Secondly, this is not about Kevin. This is about *you* finding your own path. It's about *you* living your own life."

"That sounds fine in the abstract, but what if I leave and the sales group falls apart? I can't have that on my conscience." Fiona's voice had started to rise. "I'm ruining Kevin's life by even thinking about this."

"No, you're not. Listen to yourself. You have an important role—sure—but the factory won't shut down just because you leave. C'mon, that's taking yourself just a bit *too* seriously, don't you think?"

Fiona was silent for a long moment. "You mean I shouldn't consider myself the only person in the universe who could do that job?" She could hear Emily's soft chuckle. "Sorry, I know I'm freaking out, but it suddenly feels very real."

"That's understandable. It's a big change for you, both in thinking about changing jobs, but also from being the person taking care of everyone else in your family."

"That's not fair."

"What's not fair about it? I'm just stating the facts. You came back from your business course to work at the factory so your Da would be happy, and then when your Mum got sick, you took on her care. Am I wrong?"

"No." Fiona's voice was quiet.

"Okay, so are you supposed to now take care of Kevin?"

"I guess not." Fiona paused. "But how do I untie that

knot that's been binding me to the factory, and to Liverpool all my life?"

"The first step is to give yourself permission to consider a different path. Let yourself get used to the idea. You haven't even applied for this job yet. Once you do, you'll have to wait for an actual offer. Then, with that in hand, you'll look at the positives and negatives. After all that will be the moment to talk to Kevin."

"That makes a lot of sense. Thank you."

"I'm behind you one hundred percent, whatever you decide to do. I hope you know that."

"I can't tell you how helpful it is to talk through all of this with you. Thank you."

"I'm glad. I hope we can be good sounding boards for each other on all kinds of things. That's what friends do. Let's plan another weekend in London to talk it all through once you get an offer, which I'm sure will happen, by the way."

"Don't jinx it."

"I'm hugging you from afar. Now go order a pizza and watch some *Bake Off*. That'll take your mind off things."

"Okay. Can I call you if I have questions on the application? How could I be a forty-five-year-old woman who's never officially applied for a job?"

"Of course, you can call."

"Thank you. I'm hugging you right back. Good night."

"Good night."

*****

Fiona couldn't believe it when just a week later she received an offer letter from Claude. The email said the Board would still have to give final approval, but he didn't foresee any issues with that. Somehow, she'd fooled him into thinking she was qualified enough to hire. She felt giddy and slightly hysterical.

She spent a restless night tossing and turning but knew deep down she wanted to accept it. It was time to talk to Kevin. She wanted him to understand why she was doing this. That this was about *her* being at a crossroads in her life, and not because of any negative feelings for him or the factory itself.

After several attempts to set up a dinner together, which he'd refused saying he was too busy, they'd agreed she would stop by his office at the end of the day Wednesday. Walking up the stairs, she met his assistant, Melody, coming down to head home.

"Good night, Fiona," Melody said, smiling brightly. "He's expecting you."

"Thanks. Good night." Her smile felt forced as she continued up the final steps, quietly pushing open the door of the large office. Kevin was on the phone, looking out the plate glass window over the factory floor. She stood for a moment, taking advantage of his inattention to really look at him. She saw more streaks of gray sprinkled into his dark brown hair, and noticed it looked shaggy at the back and was in need of a trim. Since Vera had left him, he'd paid little attention to his appearance.

As he turned to make some notes at his desk, she could also see new worry lines creasing his forehead. For just a moment, she thought about turning around and going back downstairs, but at that instant he looked up and smiled, waving her in.

"Yes, I know, Larry," he said into the phone. "We'll work on getting more bids next week.... Okay, I've got to run. See you next week in Birmingham."

He stood up. "Hello!" His grin took years off his face,

and she was reminded suddenly of an afternoon when they were kids, when he'd shown her a frog he'd caught in the garden. It was the same, infectious, grin, and she smiled back.

"I know you're busy, but I really need to talk to you about something. Is this a good time?"

"Yes, come on in. I'm sorry I've not been able to get away for dinner. I've been interviewing new suppliers, and I haven't had a moment to myself. Let's go down to the caf to chat. There shouldn't be too many people, and I might be able to find something to eat. I just realized I never had lunch."

Without waiting for her answer, he grabbed his keys and motioned for her to precede him out of the door, locking it behind him. They walked in silence down the three flights to the ground floor, Fiona glancing around quickly to find a seat where they would not be overheard and was relieved to see most people had left for the day.

The cafeteria was attached to the main factory floor, its wide double doors currently standing open since the machines were silent. On the far side were a variety of coffee and tea machines, as well as several vending machines for snacks. The kitchen, which was to the right, was shuttered, the trays stacked neatly outside the normal serving window. The Braxton family had always prided themselves on taking good care of their workers, and one of the benefits of working at the factory had always been that a hot lunch was provided. At one time, there'd been a graveyard shift as well, but Kevin had eliminated that as one cost-cutting measure when he took over. Their father had been everyone's best friend, but not very good with the accounts. Kevin was still playing catch up three years after his death.

They each got a cup of tea, and as Fiona went to sit down, Kevin went to the vending machines. He soon returned with a packaged sandwich and some flavored crisps, *'potato chips' as Jane would say*, Fiona thought, smiling to herself. Kevin settled himself across from her and spent a moment unwrapping the sandwich and opening the crisps.

When she felt she had his attention, Fiona cleared her throat. "So… there's been a lot happening in my life."

That's the understatement of the century, she thought.

This was so awkward. She loved her brother, but she'd never found it easy to talk to him.

Kevin looked concerned. "Is everything okay?"

Fiona nodded vigorously. "Absolutely. I'm just not sure where to begin. I guess I'll start with my trip to Paris a little more than a month ago. Do you remember?"

"I remember I was irritated, because that was right when we had that enormous order for the new headquarters building of Smith & Sons, and there was a huge delivery cockup."

"There was a *slight* mix-up," she amended, "and my team handled it just fine without me."

"Lucky break," he said grudgingly.

"How are things going otherwise?"

Kevin shrugged. "You know. Same old stuff, but bigger bills. Actually, I shouldn't say that. I'm finally seeing light at the end of the tunnel." He took a huge bite out of his sandwich.

"Really? That's great."

He reached for a couple of crisps and popped them into his mouth. "Yeah, as hard as it was to do, sending some of Da's cronies to retirement and getting in younger people has made a huge difference. Have you met Michelle? She's overseeing the guys in the warehouse, and she's already worked out how to get free advertising with some of our vendors. That's the kind of stuff that will turn this old place around."

"I'm glad to hear it. I'm happy for you, Kev, honestly."

Kevin took a slug of his tea. "What about you? Lots has happened, you were saying?"

"Yes. In Paris, I became friends with a couple of women in the cooking class I took, and one of them, Véronique, works for a chain of French grocery stores that just opened their first store in London. That's why I went to London a couple of weekends ago."

"Oh, that's right. I remember you mentioned it."

Fiona swallowed, nervous. "Well, I recently met with the guy at Véronique's store who's in charge of construction and logistics for all the stores."

Kevin grinned and wiped his mouth. "I bet you loved that! You two probably had a good natter about the ins and outs of it all. Maybe even got a couple tips, eh?"

Fiona felt a quick spark of irritation. No praise from him for how organized her team was. Instead, a complaint about the one problem situation and a snide comment. He had no idea how much she did to make sure things ran smoothly and their clients were happy. And it hurt that that he seemed to underestimate her and her abilities so badly. "I think I do a good job keeping things together here even if you don't." She tried not to sound defensive.

"I know you do. Sorry. I didn't mean to imply anything different. So, you met and talked to this guy. And?"

"I've talked to him a couple of times actually." She paused, and then, in a rush, added, "And they've offered me a job."

Kevin choked on the last bite of his sandwich, and Fiona wasn't sure if his beet-red face was the result of that or anger at what she'd said.

"Kev, stay calm," she whispered fiercely. "There are

people watching." He turned and one of the foremen waved at them from across the room.

Kevin took a gulp of his tea, visibly making an effort to calm himself. "Fiona, you can't possibly be thinking of accepting. I know I don't say it enough, but I depend on you."

"I haven't given him my answer yet."

"Is it for more money than you make here? Do you want me to match it?"

"Kev, stop and let me finish. Yes, it's more money than I make here, but money isn't the only consideration. I love what our family has built here, and I'm so proud of what you've accomplished since Da died. I don't want to jeopardize that in any way."

"Then say thanks, but no thanks to this guy."

"It's not that simple. I'm not happy here. I feel stifled. Suffocated. Not because of anything you've done. I'm just not invested in it the way you are. For me, it's always been just a job. You know that. I've told you a million times I stayed all those years for Da, and then to take care of Mum, but it's never going to mean the same for me as it does for you."

Fiona took a large gulp of tea. "Kev, the trip to Paris not only reminded me of things I've lost in my life that I want to get back, but it gave me other things, too. A new confidence in trying new things, for instance. And a reminder of how much I like exploring new places."

"You can absolutely do more traveling while still being based here. As you pointed out, you've got a great team who've proved they can handle things while you're away," Kevin said, not noticing he was contradicting his earlier concerns.

"Yes, but there's more to it than that. With Mum gone, I now feel I can leave Liverpool completely. Build something on my own."

Kevin pushed his hand roughly through his hair, making it stand on end. "Fiona, you can help *me* build something right here. That's what I've been pushing for you to think about for months. You know I'd love that."

"I know. And that's why I haven't already accepted this other job. But what Claude is offering would let me build something from the ground up, an accomplishment completely on my own." She reached out to grip his hand tightly where it lay on the table. "Kev, I'm forty-five. I've lived my whole life here, doing what Mum and Da wanted. Maybe it's time to do something for *myself* for a change."

She knew he would feel personally betrayed no matter what she said, but his comments had reinforced her own guilt and uncertainty. Was he right? Should she stay? It *was* the family legacy. She'd never be an owner at Bon Gout. She'd just be an employee.

For a moment, neither spoke.

"Fiona, I appreciate how you took responsibility for Mum's care when she had to be put into that home. With all that the factory needed, and then Vera leaving, I was at the end of my rope—and I only got through it because I knew I could count on you."

He sighed. "We've made good progress here, and the factory is finally starting to turn a little profit." His tone hardened. "But we're not there yet, and you know better than anyone how impossible those salespeople are. You're the only person who's ever been able to keep them in line." He slumped, looking defeated.

Fiona drank the last of her tea. "Kev, if I don't grab this opportunity, another may never come along. I don't want to live with that regret the rest of my life."

Kevin fiddled with the plastic packaging that had held his sandwich. "So, you're ready to leave Liverpool, and everything you've ever known? It makes no sense to me."

He stood abruptly and moved quickly toward the stairs. Fiona watched him, a part of her wanting to run after him and take it all back, but another, increasingly louder, voice urging her to jump at this chance for a new start.

She sat rigidly in place until he'd disappeared into his office. She hoped one day he would forgive her.

Chapter 29

Eight Months Later

It was the end of March and Fiona was back in Paris. She was thankful for her warm leather coat and hugged it tighter around her as she gazed at the familiar green and white checkered tablecloths. Emily took her hand and they stepped into the restaurant, where Marie greeted them warmly. She led them through to a long table at the back, its silverware and glassware gleaming in the soft light of the candles.

Fiona turned, her eyes glowing. "It's so nice to be back here. I can't believe we found a date and time where everyone could make it. This looks perfect."

"Véronique's done most of the work, getting in touch with everyone. I don't know how she does it, with all the time she spends on the new store and now on getting ready for the baby. Martine is bringing her boyfriend Julien, and Bernard is bringing Jane, of course, but also invited his son, Antoine and his wife, Julie. Véronique said that Angela hopes she can make it, and she talked to Kallie who will definitely be here."

"Does Jane know any of this?"

"I hope not. It's supposed to be a surprise."

"Véronique said she and Jean-Pierre come here quite often, but that it will be Bernard and Jane's first time."

"That first time I came with you was one of the best meals *I've* ever had." Fiona squeezed Emily's hand. "And it's still one of my favorite memories of that week."

"Come sit over here where you can jump up to greet everyone."

Fiona had only been sitting for a moment when she did, in fact, jump back up, and looking sheepishly at Emily, she waved madly at Véronique and Jean-Pierre.

"Oh, Fiona and Emily. I am so happy you're both here." Fiona noticed Véronique's coat buttons were straining slightly. "And you will be proud of me. I have not—how do you say it— 'spilled the beans' to Jane about Kallie and Angela coming. I hope Angela is able to make it."

Jean-Pierre spoke up behind Véronique. "I made a bet with her that she would have to change all the diapers for the first two months if she told Jane anything, and it seems to have worked."

They all laughed.

"By the way, you look beautiful," Fiona said and Véronique blushed.

Marie arrived with Jane and Bernard and the next several minutes were spent with greetings and hugging all around. Then, just as they were sitting down, Martine and Julien arrived, apologizing for being late and blaming Julien's motorcycle, followed closely by Antoine and his wife, Julie, and everyone stood again.

As Bernard made the introductions, Jane noticed there were still three empty seats, but when she looked at Véronique, she just shrugged and smiled.

Once everyone was again seated, the waiter appeared with two glistening buckets of Champagne. Just as he opened the first with a delicate pop, there was another flurry of activity behind him.

"Did we miss anything?" Angela said, her face slightly flushed. "Francois got caught in traffic."

From behind her, Francois retorted, "We would have been fine if someone had been ready to go on time."

"She's always late," came a third voice, and Jane jumped up, squealing as she hugged Kallie tightly, releasing her only after a long moment to hug Angela and Francois. "I can't believe you're all here!" She turned back to Véronique accusingly. "Was this your doing?"

Véronique nodded, her whole face alight. "Angela wanted to be here if we did a celebration dinner, and of course we had to invite Kallie. Luckily, I now have an easy way to get in touch with Angela." She looked toward Francois. "Monsieur Mercier.... I mean Francois." She looked flustered, and Francois waved, grinning at everyone like they were all old friends. Jane gave them all another hug, obviously overwhelmed.

Everyone sat down again and as the waiter filled their glasses, Emily stood. "Since Véronique and I chose the location for this gathering, I hope you don't mind if I start things off by welcoming and thanking everyone for coming. As you all know, we have three people here tonight who have successfully completed the full cooking course and received their *diplômes*: Jane, Bernard and Martine." She raised her glass toward all three. "Congratulations."

There was applause, and once everyone had touched glasses, Véronique stood, slightly awkward because of her size. She moved over to where Fiona was seated, urging her up as well. "Thank you all for coming. I want to also celebrate my dear friend, Fiona, who, as you know, now works at Bon Gout and is helping me to make a second London store a reality. Fiona has found us the perfect location and building and is now getting us through the mountains of British paperwork so we can actually start construction inside. I thought the French bureaucracy was bad." There were a few chuckles. "We are hopeful we can open in October in time for the holiday shopping season!" There was more clapping and shouts of congratulations.

Jane then stood. "My turn." She looked slowly around the table. "I feel so blessed. When I arrived in Paris, I didn't know what my future held. Then I found all of you." She took a moment to raise her glass to each person. "I have found new friendships and renewed old ones." She paused again, obviously overcome with emotion, and they all cheered loudly. "As you know, I chose pastry as my specialty, and I want to raise a glass to Francois' father, who inspired me those many years ago with that double chocolate *pain au chocolat!*" She looked at Francois with a special smile.

There was more clapping and people at nearby tables were turning to see what was going on. Marie took advantage of the lull to have the waiters bring the first course.

Every dish evoked conversation and debate, and also a consensus that each course was more flavorful than the last. Thomas came out of the kitchen in his chef whites to bring the dessert tray himself, with Marie close behind. He and Bernard spoke briefly, then Bernard turned back to the group.

"Thomas could not decide which dessert would be best, so he has made miniature versions of several Paris classics, though with his own choice of flavor combinations. We have éclairs made with passion fruit and raspberry, caramel tarts with chocolate cookie crusts, macarons of every variety, and napoléons, topped with Chantilly cream flavored with vanilla and orange."

They all gave Thomas a loud round of applause, effusive in their praise of how delicious everything had been.

The evening passed in a blur, the stories recounted in an eclectic mixture of French and English. Jane, Bernard, and Martine regaled everyone with stories of triumphs and disasters during the course, and Angela made Jane blush by telling a couple of stories from their early years in Boston. Even Antoine and Julie, who had been quite reserved early in the evening, told funny stories about their latest wine harvest, and Julie, who it turned out was from Dublin, sang an Irish ballad in a beautiful alto voice. Jean-Pierre did an imitation of his client, the president of Vitesse, and Francois, not to be outdone, did an imitation of the president of Bon Gout, winking at Véronique as she laughed louder than anyone else.

As the evening drew to a close, Bernard stood, tapping his glass to get their attention. "I have a feeling this is the first of many celebrations. I've gotten permission to mention one other thing to celebrate. Besides welcoming Véronique and Jean-Pierre's firstborn in a couple of months, Martine and Julien have just found out they are expecting their first baby at the end of the year!" There was loud applause from everyone.

Bernard again held up his hand. "One final announcement. Maurice Leblanc, who owns the restaurant where I work, has offered to close the restaurant for us one evening so that Jane, Martine and I can cook a delicious meal for all of you and a few other special guests. We are still working on the date but will let you know soon."

There was laughter and rowdy applause, and Jane noticed suddenly they were the last ones in the restaurant. Reluctantly, and with many thanks to the staff, they made their way out to the street.

Jane strolled slowly along, an arm linked with Bernard

on one side and with Kallie on the other. She gazed around at the throngs of people still out and about. This was, indeed, life in Paris, and more than ever, she felt sure this was where she belonged. They passed a lit window displaying small placards with property advertisements, and she stopped for a moment.

"Bernard, look at this ad for an apartment for rent in the 11th arrondissement. Maybe we should go take a look?"

Acknowledgements

This book has gone through many different iterations, and I want to thank Nellie Sabin for early editing help, and Sarah Branham, whose inciteful editing expertise and suggestions have made this a much more compelling story. Thanks also to my beta readers and listeners, in particular Gretchen, Cheryl, Betsy and the Ten O'Clock Club, who helped me through the many final edits and clarifications. Thanks to my son Chris for his aesthetic and editing help, and thanks always to my husband Peter, who never doubts there is a good story buried somewhere within all the versions that he reads.

Made in the USA
Middletown, DE
30 November 2023

44077574R00139